SOLVE-IT-YOURSELF MYSTERIES

THE Puzzling Adventures OF SHERLOCK HOLMES

Published in 2022 by Welbeck Non-Fiction Limited,
part of Welbeck Publishing Group.
Based in London and Sydney.
www.welbeckpublishing.com

A CIP catalogue record for this book is available from the
British Library

UK Hardback ISBN – 978 1 80279 091 7
US Paperback ISBN – 978 1 80279 053 5
UK eBook ISBN – 978 1 80279 202 7
US eBook ISBN – 978 1 80279 203 4

Text: Tim Dedopulos
Editorial: Chris Mitchell
Design Manager: Eliana Holder
Designer: Stephen Cary
Illustrations: Intrepidbooks.co.uk

Printed in Dubai

10 9 8 7 6 5 4 3 2 1

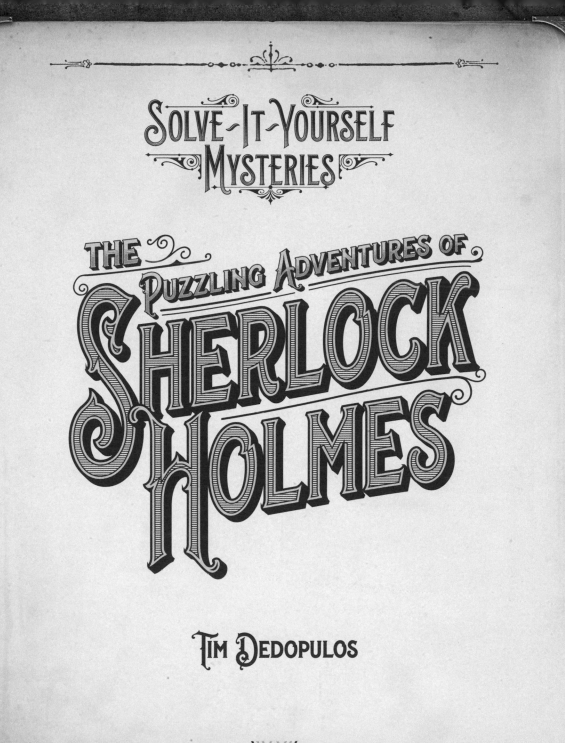

Solve-It-Yourself Mysteries

The Puzzling Adventures of Sherlock Holmes

TIM DEDOPULOS

WELBECK

Contents

INTRODUCTION

CASE 1: The Mystery of Sir Willoughby 6

CASE 2: The Flame of Bangkok 28

CASE 3: The Case of the Falling Mountain Goat ... 48

CASE 4: The Phantom of Henwood House 70

CASE 5: The Death of a Criminal 90

CASE 6: The Phantom 108

CASE 7: The Bayliss Killings 128

CASE 8: The Most Irregular Mr Wiggins 148

CASE 9: The Warden and the Coachman 168

CASE 10: The Case of the Indian Tiger 188

CASE SOLVED 208

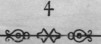

Introduction

I have been releasing detailed accounts of the more compelling exploits and investigations of Mr Sherlock Holmes to the public for some years now. It brings me great cheer that a number of persons have come to enjoy these chronicles. Holmes is my very dear friend, and whilst I am in no respect blind to the quirks of his often difficult nature, he possesses a truly brilliant mind equalled only by one or two others in this entire country. He would never seek recognition, but please know that your interest in his work does bring him a small measure of comfort in his darker hours.

I am more grateful than I can say for your nobility of spirit, my friends.

Whilst I typically present Holmes's adventures in the traditional manner of storytellers since time immemorial, I have somewhat broken with that habit for this volume. Instead of preparing the tales within as singular items, I have split them into segments. Each chapter finishes with a little test of your own powers of observation. In each instance, the truth is naturally right there on the pages you have examined, and I am quite certain that a modest degree of thought will swiftly furnish you with the correct answer. I pray that you take these little challenges in the spirit in which they are offered, that of good-natured amusement, and find some entertainment in them.

I remain your most sincere and devoted servant.

John Watson, London, 1887.

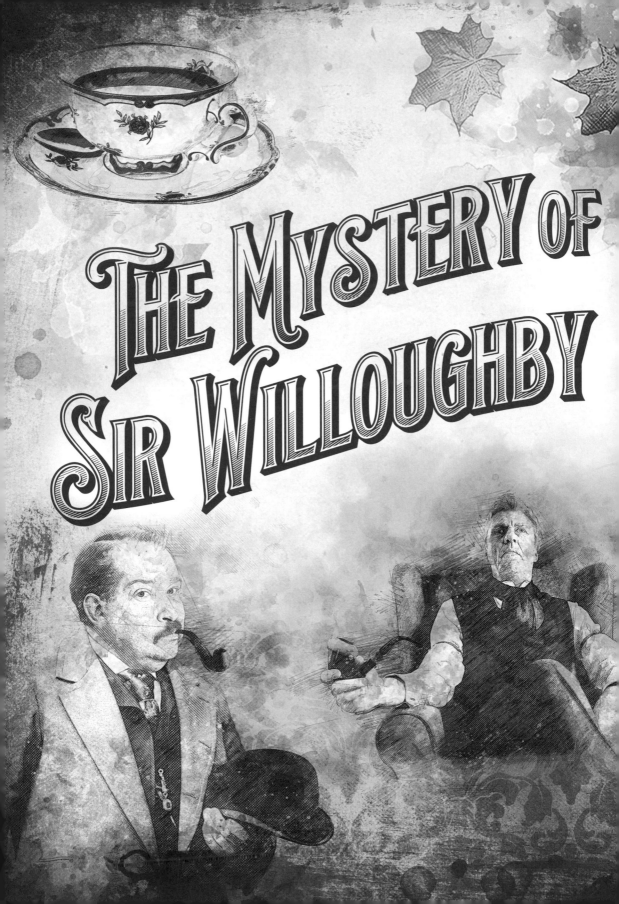

The Mystery of Sir Willoughby

THE MYSTERY OF SIR WILLOUGHBY

PART ONE

"Please do not worry, we need no solemn and binding
oaths to ensure our discretion."

It was October and, whilst it was scarcely past five in the afternoon, daylight was already fading. The wind whipped yellowed leaves and other detritus down Baker Street and, from the way the people on the street below me were hunched up, I could see it carried quite a bite. I glanced around the cosy environs of 221b and gave silent thanks that I was tucked away inside. Mrs Hudson had brought up a fresh pot of tea just a few minutes before and, as I had been too busy to have lunch that day, I resolved to indulge myself in both a second cup and a third biscuit.

I'd taken but two steps from the window when Holmes appeared from his study, clutching an envelope. I offered him a friendly smile. "More tea, old chap?"

He waved the suggestion aside. "Gather your things, Watson. I fancy it worth a little of our time to pay a visit to St James's."

I eyed the teapot and tried not to sigh. "Now?"

"Time is of the essence, my dear fellow."

"Very well."

Twenty minutes later, considerably chillier, I stood with Holmes on the eastern section of Ryder Street. Fortnum & Mason's food hall was less than a hundred yards away, and I gloomily reprimanded myself for not bringing a couple of digestives with me.

Abandoned, alas!

RYDER STREET

CITY OF WESTMINSTER   W.1.

I rather wished I was at
Fortnum & Mason's

The elegant door in front of us opened soundlessly to reveal a trim fellow in his fifties.

"May I help you, gentlemen?" His voice was pleasant, with a certain roundness to the vowels which made me think of Wales.

"Mr Sherlock Holmes and Dr John Watson to see Sir Martin Willoughby," Holmes said.

He nodded and stepped aside. "Please come in, sirs. My name is Rowlands. I will see if Sir Martin is available."

We were led through a tastefully restrained hall, where we were divested of our outerwear, and into a well-appointed reception room. We took seats at the long coffee table - an Indian piece, unless I missed my mark. Several excellent landscapes hung on the walls, including a particularly fine study of a tree-lined crossroads. A short while later, a maid came into the room, bobbed a curtsy, and deposited a tray of refreshments. Holmes assured her that we could pour our own tea, and I had just taken a bite of a deliciously mustard-laden ham sandwich when Rowlands returned with his master in tow.

I stood, swallowing hurriedly. To this day, I do not know how I managed to suppress the ensuing coughing fit. By the time my eyes had stopped watering, Rowlands had departed again, and Holmes was shaking our host's hand.

My first impression of Sir Willoughby was that he looked rather like a grocer, with a narrow, slightly pale face, thinning hair, a mild countenance and a hint of a stoop. However, he was dressed exquisitely. When he spoke, his words were tinged with pain. "Thank you so much for agreeing to meet with me, Mr Holmes."

Sir Martin Willoughby

"My apologies for not sending advance notice," Holmes replied. "I judged the matter of sufficient importance to call on you today, and I feared that a delay would have seen you already departed for Grand Lodge."

Willoughby flinched back from Holmes, visibly alarmed.

"Your letterhead identified you as a fellow of the Royal Institute. Many of the titled fellows of the Institute are Freemasons, so I judged it a likely possibility you were as well.

This lapel pin identifies you as a member of the Septimus Club and, whilst it may not be public knowledge, I am aware that its membership comes primarily from the Craft. The overlap makes your affiliation a simple deduction. Grand Lodge meets on the last Thursday in October, which is tonight. We shall endeavour to delay you as little as possible, so that you can make it to Great Queen Street in sufficient time. Please do not worry, we need no solemn and binding oaths to ensure our discretion."

"I … see," he said weakly. "I appreciate your candour and circumspection."

Holmes nodded. "Please tell us about your father's death."

"It was Sunday and, as usual, the family was gathered at our seat in Surrey. We had a pleasant luncheon and general catch-up. After tea, when we all went about our own affairs, Father retired to his study with strict orders not to be disturbed unless he called for one or another of us. He spoke to Ronald, my sister's husband, for a few minutes in the early afternoon, and to my youngest brother, Lawrence, for a similar amount of time before five. No one else, as I recall. At five twenty-five, a gunshot rang out from the study. I was just 10 feet away, and so I was the first through the door. He was slumped on his desk in a pool of his own blood, arms dangling down by his sides. He'd shot himself clean through the heart. The revolver he'd used was in the desk tidy, underneath which was a short note, clearly in his handwriting." He paused for a moment, wrestling with emotion.

A replica of the Septimus Club Pin

"What did the note say?" Holmes prompted.

"It said only, 'Please forgive me. I cannot continue.' He'd signed it, of course. But it doesn't make any sense, Mr Holmes. Father was a cheerful, good-natured man. He liked reading more than any other pursuit and spent the great bulk of his time contentedly at home with Mother, enjoying his retirement. He was neither unwell nor in debt, and I honestly can't imagine how he might have hidden some great scandal. Even if some disaster had befallen him, I greatly doubt he would ever have been so driven to despair as to take his own life. It must have been something truly shattering. None of us can think of anything. Will you help uncover the reason for Father's suicide? If there is some secret disgrace, then we must make amends."

The offending revolver – and note

Holmes shook his head impatiently. "Your father did not commit suicide. He was murdered."

Why does Holmes believe that Sir Willoughby's father was murdered?

The case continues overleaf

THE MYSTERY OF SIR WILLOUGHBY

ANSWER on page 209

THE MYSTERY OF SIR WILLOUGHBY

PART TWO

"Not impossible,
Sir Willoughby.
Merely improbable."

Willoughby stared blankly at Holmes for several seconds. "Murdered? But I was right there, in the next room. I had a clear view of the door. I dashed straight over. There was no one in the study, and nowhere for a murderer to have gone. The window was even locked, man. It's impossible."

Holmes's eyes gleamed. "Not impossible, Sir Willoughby. Merely improbable. I can think of at least a dozen ways such a thing could be done. But I will need to examine the scene myself. I assume it is no longer intact?"

Poor Willoughby was clearly in a degree of shock, but he shook his head. "No. That is, yes, your assumption is correct. After the doctor took Father away, I put the gun and note away and tidied the room with the help of Rowlands and Father's man, Baker. I didn't want anyone else to have to see. I'm sorry if that is unhelpful."

"No matter. The room will prove revealing. I think Saturday will be sufficient ... Yes. Quite sufficient. If you would be so kind as to ensure that your family is gathered at the house?"

The fellow merely nodded obediently.

"Capital," Holmes said. "Watson and I will call upon you a little after three p.m., allowing for the vagaries of the Guildford train. I am confident that this matter can be resolved in a timely manner."

"We are sorry for your loss," I added.

"Thank you," Willoughby replied automatically.

Holmes glanced at his pocket watch. "You can still be in good time for Grand Lodge so long as you instruct your driver to avoid Long Acre. Good day. Come, Watson." He strode out of the room and, with little choice, I followed.

Thursday evening passed quietly, and I barely saw Holmes on Friday. I had some early appointments to attend to, and he was out and about by the time I returned to Baker St. It would be some time before I discovered his business that day. Saturday dawned somewhat overcast but lightened during the morning. By the time we set off for Waterloo station after an early lunch, only the occasional fluffy white cloud drifted east toward Essex. The wind remained cold, though, and I was glad of my Burberry.

Apart from a short delay at Woking, we made good time to Albury Hall, the country home of the Willoughby family. It had been in the family for four generations, according to Debrett's. It turned out to be a pleasant enough red-brick pile as we approached, sprawling and well appointed but lacking any particularly distinguished architecture. A homely sort of estate, rather than one designed to impress. The extensive orchards appeared to be practical, rather than decorative, and I found myself wondering whether the family produced a cider.

Our cab deposited us outside Albury's front door at precisely ten minutes past three and, before we had climbed the three short steps leading up to it, the door opened. Rowlands,

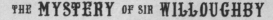

Ten past three precisely. Holmes was not always so prompt

Sir Willoughby's man, was standing there with a pleasant expression on his face. He offered us a polite half bow. "Gentlemen, Sir Willoughby welcomes you to Albury Hall."

After we'd shucked our coats and hats, we followed the fellow into the depths of the manor. The same sense of restraint that I had noticed in Willoughby's London home dominated

Rowlands, Sir Willoughby's man

here. The rooms were attractive without being ostentatious, and the artwork had been curated with a careful eye for harmony over monetary value. Holmes's work takes us to a great variety of locations, and you may believe me when I say that taste is a virtue all too often lacking in the homes of the great and the good.

Willoughby met us in a charming little occasional room a short way off the large formal dining room. He looked careworn, but otherwise hale enough. I suspected he'd not had much sleep over the past couple of nights.

"Sir Willoughby," Holmes said, nodding pleasantly. "If you would show us to your father's study?"

"Thank you for coming, gentlemen," he replied. "I'll take you there directly. As I'm sure you have anticipated, the room has been cleaned and tidied since my father's death."

"Of course," Holmes said.

Willoughby gave a weary nod and led us a down a stretch of corridor to a sturdy oak door. He paused outside and fished in his pocket for a key. "I had the room locked on Thursday night. Too little, too late, I'm quite sure, but it might have helped a little."

Holmes waited for him to open the door, then stood in the

doorway for a long moment, getting a sense of the room. I saw his eyes narrow fractionally before he stalked in.

I turned to Sir Willoughby. "Holmes typically prefers to make his examinations unprompted, Sir Willoughby," I told him quietly. "If he has questions, he will not be shy of asking them, as I'm sure you have ascertained."

"I expected nothing less," Willoughby replied, equally quietly.

As we watched, Holmes prowled around the room. The leather-bound desk was heavily bloodstained, although more so toward the edges of the stain than at its centre. He examined the blotchy mark closely. He knelt down behind the desk, beside the chair, and studied some small indentations in the carpeting before getting up. Next, he began pacing around the room, apparently scrutinizing the walls. He went straight past a rather fine hunting scene but stopped to examine a shelf of books in great detail, poked at a small hole next to the window frame but ignored a scratch in the wallpaper nearby, and rattled one of the windows looking out onto the gardens but ignored the other. He spent a moment studying the ceiling, and then turned his attention to the fireplace. After a little thought, he picked up a poker and inspected the ashes in the grate carefully with a degree of clanking and a small clink. He poked around in the ashes with his hand for a moment, then replaced the poker, sat back on his heels briefly as he wiped his fingers clean on his handkerchief, then came smoothly to his feet and turned to face us.

We waited by the door

"There was some paperwork on the desk when your father died?" Holmes asked.

"Yes, actually, there was, now you mention it. Some papers or a letter or something. Quite

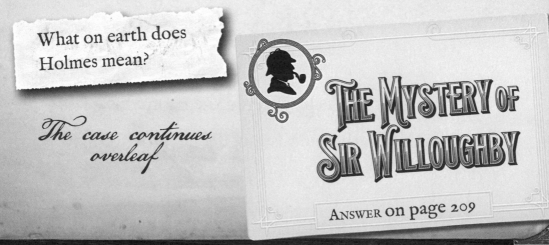

Examining the ashes

indecipherable. I'm afraid I just threw them out and forgot all about it."

"I see. And has your father been interred yet?"

Willoughby shook his head. "Not yet. He is in the care of Smith & Sons in town. The funeral is tomorrow. Many people want to pay their respects, as I'm sure you can imagine."

"Quite, quite," Holmes said. "I dare say that, if you instructed the funeral director to open your father's chest, you would find a bullet in there, but it would not have been the cause of his death."

Poor Willoughby just stared, blank-faced and pale.

"The reason you did not find the murderer when you came into the room is that your father was alone when the shot was fired. He had, however, been quite dead for some time."

What on earth does Holmes mean?

The case continues overleaf

The Mystery of Sir Willoughby

Answer on page 209

*The Honourable Sir
Justice Willoughby*

THE MYSTERY OF SIR WILLOUGHBY

PART THREE

"He flinched as he entered the room, his gaze flicking to the bloodstained desk repeatedly."

Willoughby looked at Holmes in considerable distress. "But Lawrence saw my father little more than half an hour before I found him. Surely you're not suggesting ... ?"

"I am not suggesting anything at this point," Holmes said blandly. "Merely stating fact. If we assume your father was alive when your brother went in to see him, as seems likely, then his death came at some moment between then and when you heard the bullet discharge. The precise timing is not possible to ascertain at this moment."

Willoughby nodded unhappily. "Yes. I understand."

"There might be a third party involved," I said, as gently as I could.

"Possible," Holmes said. "Quite possible. For the moment, I would like to speak to the family individually. I would prefer to conduct my interviews in here."

"I ... Is that really necessary?"

"I do not know at this time whether it is strictly necessary or not, but it might well prove decisive."

Sir Willoughby's jaw firmed and, for the first time, I saw a hint of the strength that lay beneath the bereavement and pleasant demeanour. "Yes. I can see how it might be, at that. I will send them in. Is there any particular order?"

"Lawrence first, I think. I will instruct him on who to send next."

Willoughby nodded grimly, paused on

Sir Martin Willoughby left with a firm determination

the verge of saying something, then changed his mind and departed.

"Watch the children as they come in, Watson," Holmes said, unnecessarily.

"Of course," I replied.

A few minutes later, there was a knock and a fashionable man in his late thirties or early forties came in. Where Sir Martin was understated, his youngest brother was very carefully just on the right side of ostentatious. He removed a coat to reveal an expensively flattering suit, a colourful and rich silk tie and pocket square, gem-studded cufflinks, and shoes more fashionable than comfortable. He looked perfectly respectable, but there was a strong hint of the showman beneath the surface. If he was dismayed to enter the fatal room, he hid it well.

"Thank you for speaking with us," Holmes said. "I believe you were the last person to see your father alive last week?"

"Not if what Marty tells us is true," Lawrence replied. His voice was deeper and more resonant than his brother's, with an edge of theatricality about it.

"Would you tell us what you spoke about?"

"Of course. Father was concerned about how, and what, I was doing."

"Was that a common concern?"

Lawrence frowned. "Frankly, yes. Marty is the responsible one of the four of us. He's always borne the weight of Father's expectations for us, so that Miri, Alex and I might have a little space to find agreeable paths through life. Father understood that, and accepted it even, but he still always hoped that I would be drawn to something that he considered more fitting than my typical pursuits."

Holmes nodded. "Golf."

Lawrence smiled, his face lighting up. "You know of me?"

"I fear I do not follow sports. However, you have a ridge of calluses on the edge of your right thumb, which is quite specific to the most serious and adept golfers. Given the way you stand, slightly off the balls of your feet, you spend many hours a week in play and practice. I would wager that you are quite well known in your circle."

"Indeed." He looked impressed and no less delighted. "It is the only world in which I feel truly myself. I am, if you will excuse my lack of modesty, very good indeed. Not quite great, but not far from it. There are maybe a hundred of us at or above my level. We share a companionably friendly rivalry, marvel at the half-dozen geniuses, and enjoy the admiration of our slightly less talented peers and other enthusiasts. Father never really felt it seemly. He was not, by nature, a sportsman."

"How did his mood seem when you spoke to him?"

"He was making an effort to appear in good humour, but I could see that he was pained by something. I assume that was why he'd chosen to take some time alone that afternoon. He did not volunteer any information, and I did not pry."

Lawrence Willoughby,
upon arrival

Ronald Norton,
Miranda's husband

"Thank you for your time," Holmes said. "Would you be so good as to send Ronald in next?"

Miranda's husband arrived promptly. He was a dapper man in his mid fifties, well-to-do, perhaps a little staid. There was a certain cast to his skin that suggested depression and poor sleep. He flinched as he entered the room, his gaze flicking to the bloodstained desk repeatedly, and introduced himself as Ronald Norton in a subdued, oddly flat voice.

"You're a Lloyds' Name, of course," Holmes said.

Norton nodded listlessly.

Holmes started to explain his deduction, then stopped. "Would you be so kind as to tell us what you discussed with your father-in-law last Sunday?"

He made a visible attempt to gather himself. "My father was a deeply unpleasant man, gentlemen. Miranda's father was kind and affable, and accepted me with a warmth I had never known from my own parents. I already miss him dreadfully. We talked about the future. He asked about Lloyds, and my work at the Old Lady, and seemed enthusiastic when I told him about my plans to purchase a small Dutch collection for the National Gallery. He seemed a little distracted - a little weighed down - and I assumed that was why he'd secluded himself. I didn't think to ask why. Now I never can." His quiet voice trailed off.

I offered some condolences, and Holmes dismissed the man. What turned out to be our last interviewee was the middle brother, Alexander. He was slight, with a soft voice and a studious air. Holmes identified him as an Egyptologist, based on the cotton of his shirt, a slight tan to his hands, and the design of one his rings.

"You're quite correct, sir," he said. "I am also interested in

Egyptian design

Greek and Roman antiquities, of course, but Egypt is my primary passion. I assist several of the London museums. It is a fascinating culture, and we are lucky so much of it has been preserved."

"You were not called to your father's study last Sunday. Do you know why that was?"

He shrugged. "I haven't given it any thought. It's not as if we were regularly called in here for interviews or anything."

"Was it common for your father to closet himself away in here?"

"Not especially, but it certainly wasn't unknown. Usually, he'd be reading, or perhaps sending a letter. Very occasionally there would be some case or other rearing up in his more active days. Maybe the document he was working on would have shed some light on his murder. You are sure it's murder? I have to say that it seems unlikely. Then again, it's no less unlikely than him taking his own life. It's all so strange and sad and bewildering."

"What did your father retire from, precisely?"

Alexander looked a little surprised. "He was a High Court judge."

"I see. Thank you for your time. Could you send in Sir Willoughby next?"

The man nodded, made his farewells, and departed. While we waited for Sir Willoughby to return, Holmes turned to me. "Well, Watson? There is no need to interview Miranda. I trust you know what happened now."

Who is the murderer?

THE MYSTERY OF
SIR WILLOUGHBY

ANSWER on page 209

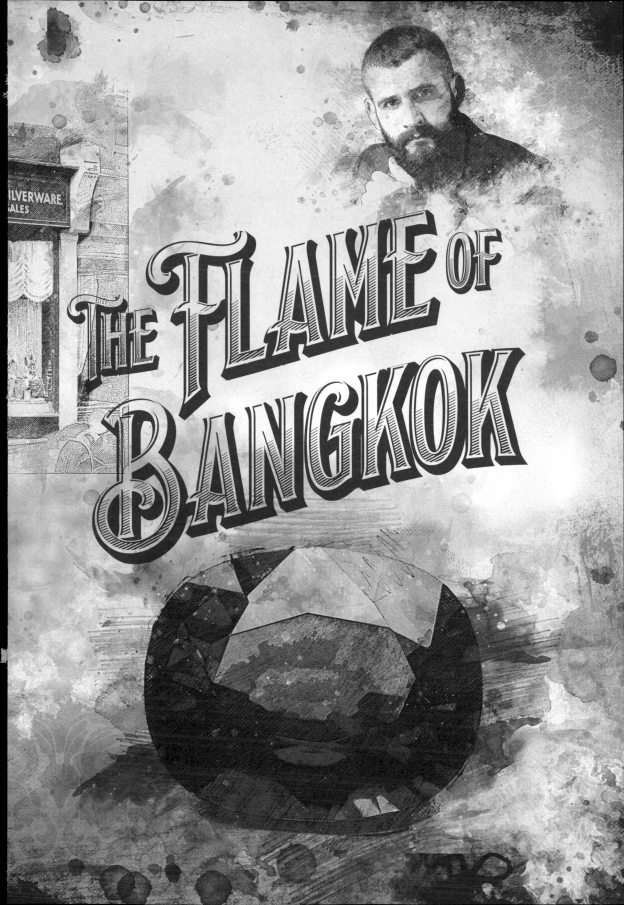

Inspector Lestrade,
a rat-faced fellow

THE FLAME OF BANGKOK

PART ONE

"You have examined the case and don't
really understand all the details."

Inspector Lestrade was a slightly rat-faced fellow, lean and possessed of a certain relentless energy. He had achieved a reputation within Scotland Yard as a man who could handle complex and sensitive cases. That reputation was almost entirely created off Sherlock Holmes's work. As his acclaim grew, the difficulty of Lestrade's typical cases rose higher and higher above his natural talent, and he leaned more and more on Holmes for assistance. Despite the potential aggravations of the situation, Holmes did not object. Lestrade's cases often required little more than a conversation, and when they led to a little more exertion, Sherlock seemed to regard the imposition as something akin to the weather - unfortunate, but not worth becoming excited about.

On a Tuesday morning in early November, Lestrade arrived unannounced, as usual, in a great deal of distress. This was less usual.

Holmes took one look at him and nodded. "The Cutler jewellery robbery in Hatton Gardens last night. The Chief Constable of Scotland Yard has spoken to you this morning and insisted that you solve the matter instantly, if not sooner, and warned that, should you fail, dire things will happen to your career. The loot that was made away with is deeply sensitive, and Cutler is well connected, so the goods must be retrieved by Thursday morning before the new Russian ambassador arrives. You have examined the case and don't

The imminent
Russian ambassador

really understand all the details, but you have some suspects."

Lestrade twitched. "Yes, Mr Holmes. In all particulars."

Holmes permitted himself a thin smile. "Well, then. Please fill me in regarding the details of the theft. Watson, if you would be so kind as to pour our harried inspector some tea?"

I poured a cup and handed it to Lestrade, who took it thankfully, sank into a chair, and drained it with a single gulp. "It's as you said, Mr Holmes. Luke Cutler is a friend of some high muckety muck and gets special jobs for the government. A very special ruby has been stolen, and it needs to be back before the Russians hear we lost it. I've spoken to Cutler. He lives above his shop, and he was relaxing after a day of work when the door alarm started ringing fit to burst. He dashed downstairs - there in less than twenty seconds, he says - but the ruby had been stolen and the place was empty. Thing is, there was a security door as was cut open, and it couldn't have been done in ten minutes, let alone ten seconds. Some of the local coppers came running within a minute or two and rounded up the people heading away from the place, but the gem wasn't on any of them."

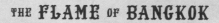

The Flame of
Bangkok

"I suppose it could be momentarily diverting," Holmes said. "I'll need to examine the scene and speak to Mr Cutler."

"He's down at the Yard right now," Lestrade said. "Our lads are guarding the shop."

Holmes nodded. "Very well. The site of the robbery will

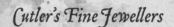

Cutler's Fine Jewellers

undoubtedly be more informative than the unfortunate jeweller."

Lestrade had a coach outside, and so we piled in and made our way to Hatton Gardens. It was a pleasant late-autumn day, bright and crisp, and I rather enjoyed the ride. When we got there, Hatton Gardens was buzzing with interested parties of bystanders, sensation-seekers, and jewellers frustrated at the sight of crowds who had not the least interest in their wares.

Cutler's Fine Jewellers was a well-maintained establishment, spick and span both inside and out. Most jewellery shops look much the same, and this one was stamped from the usual die, with plenty of space and light, glass counters, a bench with a variety of tools and instruments, and interior styling chosen for its blandly prosperous feel without detracting from the wares. Holmes glanced around and gestured for Lestrade to lead on.

We went into a back room that was cosier and far less ordered. There was a small kitchenette for staff refreshment, shelves filled with a variety of boxes and miscellaneous shop items, a closet for cleaning supplies, a couch with a comfortable-looking armchair, and a fireplace, looking forlorn in its ashy emptiness.

The steel door

The only feature that broke the comfortable feeling of the room was a heavy steel door with a big, sturdy handle and a complex-looking lock. It swung slightly open to reveal a doorway blocked by floor-to-ceiling iron rods, each one an inch thick and set no more than two-and-a-half inches apart. On the other side of this grille was a small room, no larger than the cleaning closet, consisting of dense shelving.

Holmes went over to the door and had a look at the locking mechanism. "Yes, this is quite sophisticated," he said. "Any lock can be circumvented, but this would require several minutes for even me to open. I assume the lock for the secondary security grille is only accessible

Hugh Jagger,
the enforcer

if you open the door wider." He pushed the heavy metal door wide open, then looked at the space revealed in the door frame. "There we are. This one is also as challenging, but untouched. You say some men were rounded up outside the shop?"

The inspector consulted a notepad in his pocket. "Three. They're all suspicious. Hugh Jagger is a bailiff's enforcer who lives and works in Bethnal Green. I suspect he's doing a bit of illegal prizefighting on the side. Reuben Folkson is a stevedore who lives in Whitechapel. I'm fairly confident he was gambling. Frederick Chapman is a builder from Clapham, and his clothes are too expensive for his profession. They all have plausible reasons for being in the area, at least on the surface. I have men checking out their stories, of course. Would you like to talk to them now?"

"I very much doubt that your suspicious fools had anything do with this."

Why does Holmes think that the suspects are innocent of the robbery?

The case continues overleaf

THE FLAME OF BANGKOK

ANSWER ON page 211

THE FLAME OF BANGKOK

PART TWO

"For many criminals, I have no doubt that the sight

is the stuff of quite literal nightmares."

Lestrade nodded glumly at Holmes's pointed comments regarding big arms and small apertures. "They're beefy lads, that's for sure," he said. "I guess that puts us back at square one."

"Not in the least," Holmes said. "Look at the bars here. They've been wiped clean, but there are telltale smears of grease on two of the bars here." He pointed toward the left side of the grille. "That tells us that the thief's arm is not unusually thin, yes, but also that he or she knew enough to come prepared. That restricts our suspect pool considerably on its own. Now, look at the safe room itself."

We looked at the small room obediently. The shelves were quite full, but the items on them were curiously uniform. Around three quarters of the items were identical cases, dark and sturdy, about a foot in length, half a foot in width, and maybe two inches in height. The rest were small pouches, made of some felted cloth, brown in colour. Some appeared fuller than others, but there was precious little to distinguish them. Given the space taken up by the shelving, there was enough room for a man to stand in there with the door closed, but little more.

Holmes looked at us expectantly.

"He had to know what he was looking for," Lestrade answered.

"Good," Holmes said.

"Well, I dare say I can work with that. But I still don't know how he, or she, Mr Holmes, vanished into thin air."

"I will need to speak to the unfortunate Mr Cutler," Holmes said. "I have a suspicion, but I would like to hear his recollection of events."

"We'll have to pay a visit to Scotland Yard, then," Lestrade said. "I suppose I'll have those chaps we rounded up released at the same time."

We followed the inspector out of the shop and down Hatton Gardens to the space where Lestrade had left his coach. As

The felt pouches

we made our way through the centre of London down toward Victoria, I turned to Holmes. "Why do you think there's all this hoo-ha about a jewel theft, old chap?"

Sherlock eyed Lestrade mischievously. "Oh, that's clear enough."

The inspector twitched violently. "The matters surrounding this case—"

"Are perfectly clear," Holmes interjected. "As we are in no way sworn to secrecy, engaging in speculation breaks no confidences."

Lestrade sighed, his expression glum. "As you like, Mr Holmes."

"It is thus, Watson. The Russian ambassador undoubtedly presented the crown with a very impressive ruby, with the regards of the Tsar. Naturally, Her Majesty assured him that she would have it worked into a most elegant setting, possibly as part of an ornate necklace. I happen to know that the fellow returns from the continent tomorrow, and word is that there is to be a reception at the palace on Friday. Therefore, Her Majesty intends to wear the gem then and would be dreadfully embarrassed by its absence."

Across from us, Lestrade huffed, but said nothing.

Some minutes later, we arrived at Scotland Yard. It's an impressive bastion, all imposing architecture and stout gates, swarming with constables and other officers of the law. For many criminals, I have no doubt that the sight is the stuff of quite literal nightmares. With Lestrade accompanying us, we were whisked into the

*Her Majesty
The Queen*

building and through a series of tediously institutional corridors and stairways. We ended up at a pleasant enough interview room, one of the places they keep for victims and well-regarded witnesses, rather than for suspects. I have, from time to time, seen the latter, and they are far less welcoming.

Lestrade left us there and returned a few minutes later with a short, slender man whom he introduced as Lucas Cutler. Mr Cutler looked tired and careworn, and his clothes suggested that he had received very little sleep the previous night. His expression was dark, but there was a clear curiosity in his eyes. He was followed into the room by a stolid policeman, who deposited a tray containing cups, milk, sugar and a jug that, by the smell, held rather over-brewed coffee. Once the tray was down, the policeman retreated, closing the door behind him.

"Mr Cutler, this is—" began Lestrade.

"Mr Sherlock Holmes," Cutler said. "Sir, I have followed the stories of your career with interest. It is an honour, and it gladdens my heart to see that you are involved in this investigation."

"You're far too kind, Mr Cutler," Holmes said, but he was clearly pleased to be recognized. "We have looked around your establishment, and it provides some answers, but I would be grateful if you would tell us in detail about the robbery and the events preceding and following it."

Cutler nodded. "Of course. Before the alarm sounded, yesterday had been quite typical. Quiet morning and afternoon, separated by a reasonably busy lunchtime period. Deliveries at ten in the morning and three in the afternoon, as scheduled. I was working in the back for the majority of the day, preparing some settings." He glanced at Lestrade, then back to Holmes. "As well as some other bits and pieces. I make almost all of the work we sell, but I am not a lapidary, so I either buy gems already cut, or send rougher stones down the street to Llewellyn Falconer. The man is a genius. Anyway, I made sure everything was stowed away and took over the shop floor at around four p.m. We had a few customers, the usual late-evening traffic, and I started

The helpful Lucas Cutler

shutting up at six thirty. I don't lock up until I'm the only one left in the place. The procedure is second nature at this point. Shutter the windows and lock the door, then take the display cases from the windows and the shop's displays, move them to the vault, bring up the hydraulic bars, lock the mechanism, seal and lock the vault doors and, finally, douse the lights. I keep the only keys to both the vault locks around my neck at all times. I suppose they could be duplicated, but they'd have to be stolen from me first. After locking up, I went upstairs and started preparing my supper. About forty-five minutes later, the alarm went off. It's damnably loud, I'll tell you that. Startled the devil out of me. I abandoned my kedgeree, grabbed my shotgun and charged downstairs. To my bewilderment, the front door was

The sadly abandoned kedgeree

closed and the back room was peaceful. I could see that the vault door was open, but there wasn't a soul to be seen. By the time I'd done my nervous sweep of the place, a bobby had arrived, and I could hear the whistles of more not so far behind him. That's when I discovered that the F ... the stone had been stolen from where I'd put it that afternoon. I understand why it was targeted, of course, and I can imagine someone skilled hiding from me and slipping out when my back was turned, but I really am baffled as to how someone could get in, crack the vault and steal the stone in the twenty seconds it took me to come down the stairs."

Holmes nodded approvingly. "You have a good eye for detail, sir. It was a simple matter."

How does Holmes think that the thief pulled off the robbery so quickly?

The case continues overleaf

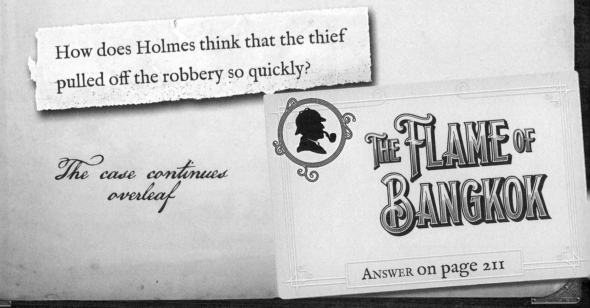

THE **FLAME** OF **BANGKOK**

ANSWER on page 211

THE FLAME OF BANGKOK

PART THREE

"This is a matter of crown interest, Mr Holmes.

It's important to stop rumours spreading."

While Luke Cutler quietly absorbed the impact of what he had been told, Holmes turned his attention to Lestrade. "My dear fellow, I assume you have a list of the staff who work for Mr Cutler, or who have done so in the reasonably recent past?"

"Of course," Lestrade said, sounding slightly offended.

"Mr Cutler," Holmes said. "Are there any people on that list of Lestrade's whose arms are sufficiently wide as to rule out reaching through the bars of your vault?"

Cutler pulled himself together. "Morris Bowyer and Percy Turner. Percy helps me with the shop on Saturdays, and he's as strong as an ox. Morris works weekdays, usually from ten to close, and he's a beefy fellow. Very deft touch, though."

Percy Turner

Morris Bowyer

"Thank you," Holmes said pleasantly. "Let's start with the others, Lestrade. Given the sensitivity and surreptitious nature of this case, I assume you have them all detained here on variously flimsy pretences?"

Lestrade stiffened a little. "This is a matter of crown interest, Mr Holmes. It's important to stop rumours spreading. This operation has been sanctioned at the—"

"Yes, yes. Bring them one at a time to a room where Watson and I can speak to them alone, if you would."

Five minutes later, we were safely ensconced in a smaller and notably less pleasant interview room, although it was still not actively threatening. A couple of minutes after that, the first of the staff arrived.

Poppleton & Sons delivery

Nicholas Rawlings was a tall, slim man with a slightly effete air and a certain wary intelligence about the eyes. He did not seem put out to be meeting with us, and answered Holmes's questions with equanimity.

"Yes, sir, I was working yesterday. I typically tend the shop floor from opening, eight a.m., through to lunchtime. It seemed a reasonably uneventful morning, honestly. We had a delivery of metals in the morning, around ten thirty, perhaps. One of the men from Poppleton & Sons. They supply a lot of Hatton Gardens with precious metals, and we see all their delivery chaps regularly. I don't actually know his name, I'm afraid, but, yes, I could certainly identify him on sight. I'm sure R&S could whistle him up for you if you asked. Anyway, that all went smoothly. I left at two p.m., as Mrs Campbell was arriving. That's when I normally take my leave, unless Mr Cutler needs a bit of extra assistance. I went home to change, and then I headed to the Hendon bowling green. I was on the roster to referee yesterday, so I was out on the green from three p.m. to seven p.m. or so."

The next fellow in was Edmund Gregson, a slight, wiry man of a little under average height. He possessed a calm and collected manner, and I got the feeling it was habitual. He, too, seemed to take no exception to Holmes's questioning.

"My working hours vary somewhat according to Mr C's needs. Yesterday, I was in at nine to work the shop floor with Nick. I left at four p.m. I have a regular Monday cribbage game with my friends at the Dog and Duck on Grey's Inn Road. I was there before five, and there I stayed until nine or so. The working day was normal, as I recall. We had a standard delivery a little after ten, and a courier I didn't recognize brought a package in for Mr C a bit before three. Apart from twenty minutes for my sandwiches at twelve, I was on the floor all day. It's always a little busier from twelve thirty through to two, and we sold a few pieces. Rings, necklaces, brooches, nothing special."

The third clerk, Baden Tucker, was in a significantly poorer mood. He was one of those chaps who's always moving restlessly, tapping or bouncing a leg, or fidgeting with something, and his impatience bled into his manner, but he did answer Holmes's questions.

"Yes, of course I work for Lucas Cutler. I'm his factor. You do know what that means, I hope? Well, good for you. Yesterday, I was in Southend - Southend, of all places! - the entire day. A Dutch dealer wanted to ... well, it doesn't really matter what he wanted, does it? The simple fact is I was there with three other men, haggling against each other for pearls and

Monday cribbage

The coastal town of Southend

nacre, from ten in the morning all the way through until six, not allowing for two hours of badly sprung coaches each way. Of course, I got the pearls. I'm good at my job. But as thanks I'm dragged in here before I've even had a full night's sleep. It's not good enough, do you hear?"

The last person Lestrade had for us was the cleaner, Edith Campbell, a wry woman in her late thirties who reminded me unsettlingly of one my sterner anatomy professors. She seemed quite amused by the proceedings, which was a pleasant change after the irritable Mr Tucker.

"I do four dozen gentlemen on Hatton Gardens, yes. Mr Cutler is scrupulous. He's my two-to-three slot every weekday, and if I can't make it, I send my Shirley in my stead. 'Can't be selling baubles from a filthy pit, Mrs Campbell!' he likes to say. Yesterday was a normal enough day. I arrived, dusted, swept, mopped, polished the cases, bleached a few rags, put everything away, and was out in fifty-seven minutes sharp to

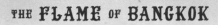

head over the way to Señor Rosa. Odd? Well, it was hardly 'odd', but there was a bit of a fuss when a sharp-dressed lad arrived with a small package. Two forty-five, that was. Mr Cutler leapt up like he'd been goosed, thanked the lad profusely, signed at least three pieces of paper, then scurried into his secure room. He came out calm again, tipped me a cheery wink, and settled back to working on a piece behind the cash desk out front. Apart from that, it was all completely normal."

Once she'd been thanked and had departed, Holmes looked at me. "You did identify our thief, didn't you, Watson?"

Who does Holmes think stole the gem?

ANSWER on page 211

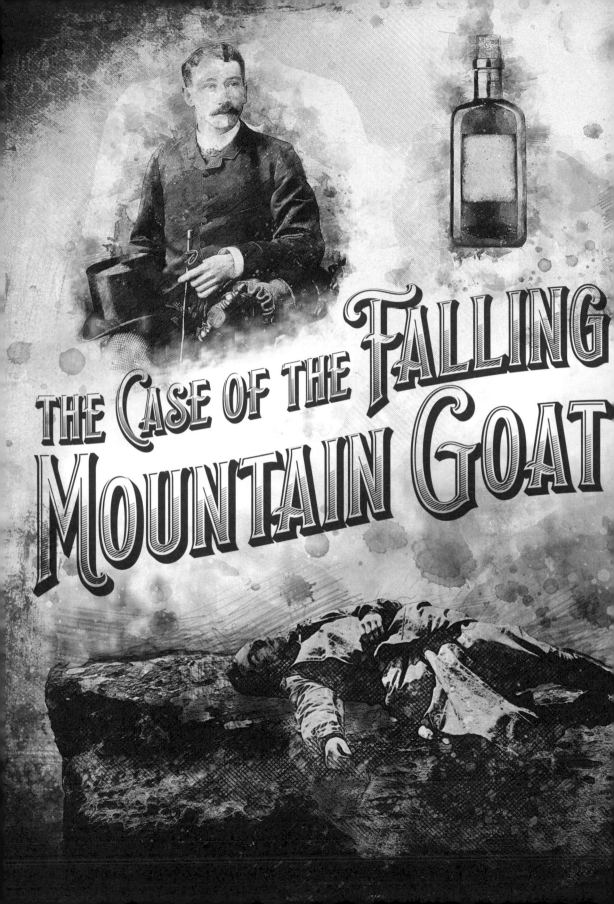

THE CASE OF THE FALLING MOUNTAIN GOAT

PART ONE

"He returned time and again to favourite sites. It was on one of these that he died."

Vincent Forster arrived at our rooms at 221b Baker Street looking careworn and exhausted. Holmes had said that he expected as much from the tone of the man's letter, but still, no doctor can see someone so obviously afflicted without a pang of sympathy. Despite his fatigue, he had contrived to ensure that his appearance was immaculate, from the crispness of his bow tie to the creases of his trousers. It was simultaneously noble and pathetic, and I warmed to fellow's plight immediately.

Once he was seated, with a fortifying cup of tea at his side, Forster started speaking in a slow, heavy voice. "Thank you for your kindness, gentlemen. My brother Enoch died just a few

Poor Vincent Forster, a cup of tea at his side

days ago, and I fear greatly that his death was no accident. The police, however, are completely uninterested. He was a climber, and a fall killed him, so that must, of necessity, be the long and the short of it. A footnote in a local newspaper about a failed climb is the most attention the world has paid. I can see how I must seem a grief-maddened sibling, unwilling to face harsh truths, but I have excellent reason to believe otherwise."

Holmes nodded. "Please, tell us the details."

"Yes, of course. Although I went into the family trade, I am—"

"A tailor," Holmes interjected. "The telltale pinpricks on your finger pads are quite distinctive, as is the precision of your deportment. The elegant fit that your clothes possess are the mark of either professional skill or a significant amount of money but, if you will forgive the observation, your shoes and watch are considerably less expensive than the expertise of your jacket would suggest. Your profession could not be plainer if you wore a sign around your neck."

Mr Forster blinked, then rallied himself. "Thank you for your generous appraisal of my skill. My family have been gentlemen's tailors for four generations. There was never any question as to my following them. I was stitching scraps together with blunt needles at the age of four, quite unprompted, to make pirate flags. Enoch, however, was cut from a different cloth. My mother's family were stonemasons, and Enoch's leanings were in that direction. He loved stone in all its varieties - collecting it, working it and, alas, climbing it. We used to joke that he was part mountain goat." He trailed off, his voice at the edge of breaking.

Enoch, in full climbing regalia

"He was a skilled climber then?"

"An expert, yes. When chance permitted, he would take himself off to the continent to scale alps, or up to Scotland to tackle the peaks there.

52

THE CASE OF THE FALLING MOUNTAIN GOAT

He talked often of a grand trip to the subcontinent, to at least see some of the great mountains said to be there. But as well as ambitious climbs, he made weekly trips to climb more local cliffs and escarpments, despite their modest challenge. It was his most beloved pastime and he returned time and again to favourite sites. It was on one of these that he died." Again, his voice died away.

"You were nearby, I understand," Holmes prompted.

"Yes. There is a pleasant tea shop near the cliff in question, on the edge of the Sussex Downs. The area is picturesque, so the shop is rarely quiet. Climbers and their friends and family are a common part of the clientele. The cliff itself, called Gibson Rock, is apparently quite straightforward. It looks hellish to me - a hundred feet of vertical insanity - but amongst enthusiasts, it is considered little more strenuous than crossing

Gibson Rock

the road. Enoch liked it because the view from the top, over the Downs, was spectacular but exclusive. The only other way up to the summit is through at least a mile of steeply rolling woodland, you see. I'd been in the tea shop for about half an hour when I heard a hubbub coming from the direction of the climb. Fearing the worst, I dashed out. I quickly gathered there had been a death. Then I got there and saw ... " His face paled even further and, for a moment, I feared he might be sick.

"Any detail might be important," Holmes said, but his voice was sympathetic.

"I, ah, I haven't spoken of this, not even to my father." Forster swallowed visibly. "It is too horrible. But I will try. Enoch ... He lay on top of a heap of rope, his body shattered. Blood covered everything. The force of the fall ... his limbs had actually separated from his torso to scatter down the rope pile

Perished on the rocks, albeit a slightly less gruesome picture than was described to us

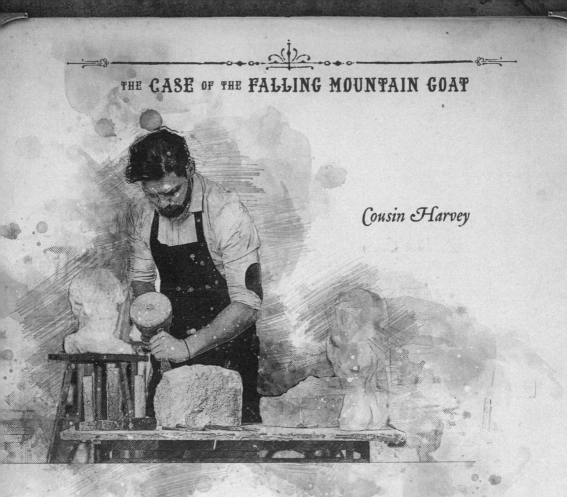

Cousin Harvey

and, whilst his head was still attached, his throat had split open."
He paused, dismay written all over him. "I collapsed, I fear. I
recall nothing more of that day."

Holmes nodded thoughtfully. "And why do you suspect
foul play?"

"You mean apart from the fact that my brother was far
too skilled to fall from a simple cliff he knew like the back of
his hand?"

"Just so," said Holmes. "Did he have enemies or business
rivals?"

"No. Stonecutting is strenuous work, but it is not exactly a
cutthr ... that is, a savage business. London is hungry for worked

Harvey's tools

stone, and prices are broadly standardized at this point. But his partner in the company is our cousin, Harvey. He's always been a passionate, tempestuous chap, but his mood has been quite sour for the last year or so. He had a very serious argument with Enoch a few days before the fall. They were throwing insults at each other in front of the whole firm, and the row ended with Harvey menacingly intoning, 'You'll regret this, you short-minded cretin,' and stalking off. That was five days ago, and now my brother is dead. Harvey is not a bad man at the heart of it, but I have no doubt that he would be capable of murder if sufficiently incensed."

"Were you able to determine the reason for the argument?" Holmes asked.

"Not clearly, but I have not tried too hard. Some difference of opinion in how to take the business forward, but that is all I know."

"I see," Holmes said. "I will pay a visit to your cousin and see what I can learn."

Forster's face lit with the first glimmers of hope. "You'll help? You believe me?"

"I have no truck with beliefs," Holmes said. "Your brother was murdered, and that fact is as clear as you sitting here today."

Why does Holmes think that Enoch was murdered?

The case continues overleaf

THE CASE OF THE FALLING MOUNTAIN GOAT

ANSWER on page 212

THE CASE OF THE FALLING MOUNTAIN GOAT

PART TWO

"I say one more time,
that filth will kill you."

58

Enoch Forster's cousin and business partner, Harvey Danton, lived on a pleasantly leafy street in Pimlico. His home was on the ground and basement floors of one address within an attractive white arcade with colonnades and other classical stylings. A communal garden ran behind the arcade - a confection of trees and flowerbeds and lawns. They looked a little barren and forlorn in the late November sun, but they were undoubtedly magnificent in the warmer months.

Danton met us at the door and invited us in politely enough. He was a scrawny chap, all skin and bones, with shadows under his eyes and a certain sallowness of his skin that suggested ongoing health issues. His features bore a hint of worn-in impatience, and it occurred to me that I could quite easily see the man losing his temper.

He led us through the house to a day room, where he'd laid out some iced water in preparation for our visit. The dominant decorative feature was Egyptian statuary. Idols, columns and stelae appeared on every

An Egyptian preoccupation

flat surface of note, and several of the walls bore large, thin slabs of stone covered in Egyptian cartouches. The effect was a little unsettling, as if we had stepped out of solid, Christian England and into some older corner of the world ruled over by the half living. Holmes flicked his eyes over it all but appeared as unmoved as ever.

We declined refreshment and sat ourselves in comfortable chairs facing Mr Danton.

"Thank you for meeting with us," Holmes began. "I would like to ask you about the rather public argument you had with Mr Forster last week."

Danton sighed, his features creasing for a moment. "Enoch. Yes, we fought. It wasn't the first time, and I'm quite sure it wouldn't have been the last. You know that we are stonemasons, I assume?"

Holmes nodded.

"It is a solid business, with no pun intended, but it is not one that has much possibility of growth. There is plenty of demand, but at a set price and, thus, a set profit. Shipments are of a size limited by cargo capacity. Expansion is possible if one buys one's own conveyances - wagons, ships, maybe both - but that is a huge hurdle to overcome. Other firms, backed or run by the very wealthy, are expanding and, sooner or later, we will be forced out of the market. It is plain. I wanted to move into more detailed work, bespoke design, perhaps even sculpture and statuary. But Enoch was far too conservative and he never did see a risk posed by the future until it bit him. He enjoyed dressing slabs, and the work was paying well enough for now, so that was that."

"So you do admit that there was significant conflict between you," Holmes said.

Danton's expression darkened, his voice becoming increasingly cold and hostile. "Obviously. Only an utter moron would deny a fact that is simple public knowledge, and I dislike the implication for my mental faculties. Furthermore, I do not appreciate the perfectly clear implication that I murdered my cousin. I know what Vincent believes. I have no idea whether that is true or not but, if Enoch was killed, it was absolutely nothing to do with me. I do know, however, that it takes a certain bloodless gall and a lack of breeding to come into a man's home and casually accuse him of slaughtering a family member. That alone tells me everything that I need—"

He broke off his increasingly vituperative tirade with a gasp, which rapidly turned into a deep, hacking cough. The cough continued, worsening, preventing him from drawing breath at all. I rose to my feet, alarmed for the fellow's immediate prospects.

He looked at me and waved at a cabinet across the room. "Liniment,"

Danton in the midst of a coughing fit

he choked. At the same time, he pushed himself off his chair to sprawl on the floor, where he stretched himself out, trying to calm his spasms and snatch tiny sips of air between coughs.

I dashed over to the cabinet and found, to my astonishment, a bottle of ABC Liniment, a thoroughly toxic substance sold by hucksters who prey on the desperate and credulous. Its chief constituents, from which it takes its name, are aconite, belladonna and chloroform - deadly poisons, all. It kills far more people than it ever aids.

I turned back toward Danton, leaving the bottle where it sat.

Fortunately, his prone position and careful breaths were starting to prevail. I checked his position and took his pulse, which was high but not frighteningly so, and poured a glass of the ice water for him to sip from when he was able to sit up.

In a few minutes, he was fully recovered from his exertions, and his wrath had also faded. Before he and Holmes could resume their discussion, however, I had to hold forth on the topic of the fatal liniment.

"You are an asthmatic," I said, careful not to phrase it as a question.

He nodded.

"That liniment will kill you faster than asthma will." I spoke as bluntly as possible. "It finishes off hundreds of unfortunates a year in England alone. If you value your life, throw it out."

The fellow blinked and looked as if he was about to protest, but he held quiet.

I lowered my tone to one of subtle menace: the voice I use with recalcitrants who shy away from stopping the activities that are killing them. "The chloroform within it might offer a slight benefit in easing your chest, but even chloroform on its own would be far too dangerous to toy with. It is easily fatal. The other two components are of absolutely no help for your condition but are every bit as dangerous. I say one more time, that filth will kill you."

He blinked again.

I moved to my calm, encouraging voice. "You would be well served by moving from

A medicine most foul

62

London to the home counties, sir, despite the disruption. Move your firm with you. When an attack approaches, I most urgently recommend a mug of very strong coffee. It's not exactly the healthiest regimen but it will help minimize the effects, and it won't kill you. If you get desperate during a stronger attack, an intoxicating measure of opium will ease the symptoms and permit your lungs to work with less opposition. You can keep a syringe on your person. But please remember that opium is extremely habit-forming, and ruinous to both body and soul if permitted to take hold of you. It should be an emergency measure only. I do sympathize with your plight, sir. You labour under a cruel ailment. But ABC Liniment is a crueller response, and even becoming an opium slave will be less fatal than using that poison."

He stared at me, a picture of wordless dismay, then nodded again. "Thank you, doctor. I take your advice most seriously, I promise."

"We are not here to bedevil you, sir," Holmes added. "We seek only to learn the truth of your cousin's murder."

Danton pinched the bridge of his nose. "I know, and I do apologize for my response. I am easily provoked right now. The ridiculous thing is that the tension between Enoch and I had been eliminated again. After our fight, we had a long, frank and measured discussion, and I managed to demonstrate to his satisfaction that our current path would bring eventual disaster. He agreed to our change of direction, and even persuaded me of the benefits of doing so at a measured pace. We were in accord, gentlemen. Our relationship was always stormy - we were very different people - but it was genuinely strong, and I valued the way that he grounded my occasional impetuosity. I will miss him."

"Have no fear on our part," Holmes said. "I know you were not the killer."

Why does Holmes believe Danton to be innocent?

THE CASE OF THE FALLING MOUNTAIN GOAT

ANSWER on page 213

The case continues opposite

THE CASE OF THE FALLING MOUNTAIN GOAT

PART THREE

"He would have hated the thought of dismemberment. What a cruel fate."

Vincent Forster took the news of Danton's innocence with surprising grace. I had anticipated some dismay but, instead, he looked positively thankful. I must have allowed some of the puzzlement to show on my face because he turned to me and said, "It is a relief to know that my cousin is not my brother's murderer, doctor. Whilst it does not bring me any closer to knowing the truth of what happened, it does at least give me some comfort. My mother and my uncle would have suffered even more terribly had Harvey been involved."

"Of course," I said, abashed.

Holmes came to my rescue. "Our next step should be to speak to Enoch's friends. There is every chance that one of them might have been taken into his confidence if he had reason to suspect that someone might seek to take his life. I feel justified in presuming that you had mutual friends, given your closeness, and I likewise feel it probable you would have mentioned if one of them had known anything possibly useful, so we can restrict ourselves to those of his friends you are not close to."

"I see the sense in that," Forster said. "Enoch had several friends in Stoke Newington, where he lived. I have met them on occasion, but they are acquaintances at best."

"Capital," Holmes said. "You can furnish us with addresses, I trust."

It took a day or so for Forster to find his brother's address book and compile a list of the individuals most likely to have been taken into Enoch's confidence. The next Saturday found us descending on Stoke Newington with a series of appointments to speak to four of Enoch's closer friends. It is a pretty area on the outskirts of London with a number of attractive and desirable properties and plenty of green space, so it is popular with the up-and-coming. At the same time, it retains a generous amount of more affordable housing, so there is a vibrancy often absent in purely wealthy areas.

Enoch's address book

The first friend, an actuary named Louis Baxter, met us in a tea shop on the edge of the common. He was a tall man in his early thirties with an open, pleasant expression and tidily

prosperous clothes. "Poor Enoch," Baxter told us. "He was a lovely man. He reminded me a little of a golden retriever, you know. Enthusiastic, optimistic, boundlessly energetic. We ran together most nights - usually laps around the Common. He needed the physical relief as much as an alcoholic needs his gin. He would have hated the thought of dismemberment. What a cruel fate. He never spoke to me of any enemies or gave me any reason to believe that he thought he might be in danger. With that said, however, he did win an oddly contentious foot race last month. The favourite failed to perform to his usual standard and, afterwards, got quite bitter, insisting he had been drugged. He didn't quite accuse Enoch, but everyone knew what he was implying."

The second friend was named Harold Sanderson. He was very tall and slightly stooped, with an apologetic air. He was clearly unsettled by our questions, but he did give the appearance of attempting to be of use. "Yes, Enoch was a good friend. We were in the rowing club together at school. He was popular and active, in ways that I was not. We meet ... met ... on Tuesdays at The Londesborough to share a few drinks.

The unsettled
Harold Sanderson

Sometimes Arthur Shearer would join us. Enoch seemed happy with life. Things were going well for him, or at least so he said. There was that fuss with the angry runner, but that had blown over and Enoch found it all highly amusing. I can't think of anything to tell you. I don't know who'd want to hurt him or why."

Charley Tennyson was a dentist, with the slightly fussy and officious mannerisms often common to the profession. He was a little older than the other two, perhaps as much as late thirties. He seemed affable enough. "Enoch and I used to golf, sometimes making a four with Louis Baxter and one of his insurance pals. Neither of us was particularly good at golf, but it is a pleasant way to get some air on a weekend. I always rather felt it was a little calm for Enoch, but he seemed to enjoy it. He did hate to sit still. I did his teeth and, even in the chair, he was always fidgeting. Fit as a badger, of course. No surprise with all that running and climbing and what have you. There's plenty of time for chit-chat on the golf course, and Enoch had been hinting at possible news, but

Arthur Shearer, in need of some cheering up

nothing more. Certainly no suggestion of anything worrying him. I can't imagine why anyone would want to do him in."

The last friend, Arthur Shearer, was a lugubrious fellow, with crow's feet that suggested his doleful mien was habitual, rather than recent. He was in his mid forties and it transpired that he was another stone man from a firm with premises near Forster's. "I heard about the argument between Enoch and Harvey, of course. They often had impressive barneys, and his lads were always sharing juicy titbits with mine over the fence. Enoch told me afterward, over a hand or five of Russian whist, that they were going to refocus, slowly, slowly. It makes sense. I've been thinking about diversifying myself. Not into decorated stone, but maybe into sands and cement. I can't image anyone killing him. It would be like slaughtering a baby deer. He was naturally popular, effortlessly companionable, and pleasant. People like that don't inspire murder. It doesn't make any sense."

We talked for a bit longer with Shearer after that, but got nothing of any use. He left us, if anything, sadder in demeanour than he had been when he arrived. We were back in the tea shop on the Common, and I found it easy to picture this energetic, hearty man running cheerfully around the grounds. It didn't make any sense to me at all, and I said as much to Holmes.

He looked at me with a certain archness. "Oh? I rather thought you might have realized that we know precisely who killed Enoch Forster."

What had Holmes noticed that I had not?

THE CASE OF THE FALLING MOUNTAIN GOAT

ANSWER on page 213

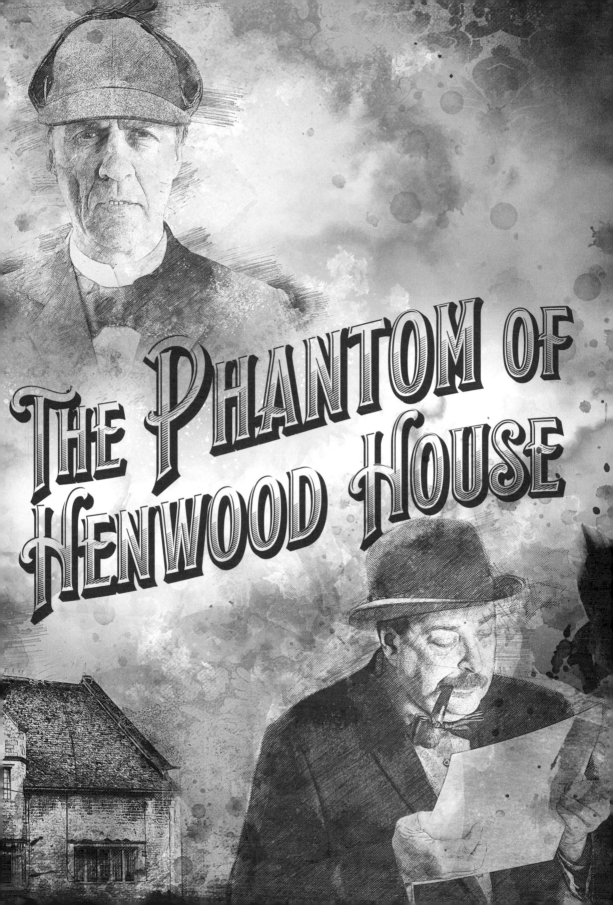

THE PHANTOM OF HENWOOD HOUSE

PART ONE

"Thank you so much for coming.

Something is very wrong here."

Sherlock Holmes was not accustomed to making house calls. Given that the majority of queries directed to him proved to be far too simple to warrant his time and attention, travelling out to interview all his potential clients would have taken more hours in the day than a whole week could afford. Sometimes, Holmes would reply to a query with a terse explanation of the solution but, more commonly, would-be cases of no interest or of obviously mendacious intent received the briefest of return notes stating that, regretfully, the matter was not for him.

Occasionally, however, a letter managed to both engage Holmes's restless curiosity and also convey sufficient urgency that he felt it important to visit the correspondent in question. So it was with the letter that Miss Gwendoline Redvers sent to Holmes one morning in early December. I read it as well, of course. In summary, it spoke of a sick father, seemingly spectral apparitions, and unlikely figures around the grounds of the Redvers house. Miss Redvers was quite convinced that her father was in imminent mortal peril, a fear which, apparently, he did not share. I'm not precisely sure which combination of factors it was that persuaded Holmes that we should take a trip out to the Meon Valley but, the next morning, we set forth. Perhaps he merely sought to alleviate his ennui.

The Meon Valley is a rather lovely area of eastern Hampshire, carved out by the winding river that gives the region its name. Henwood was a tiny village near the river: no more than a drift of half a dozen cottages. So far as I could tell, it owed its existence to our destination, Henwood House. Like the village, the house was a modest affair, as these things

Mr Sherlock Holmes
221B Baker Street
London

73

go - maybe six bedrooms for the family, accommodations for staff, a smattering of other rooms for living, dining, reception and so on, and a few acres of land, mostly turned to pasture for sheep. Well beyond the reach of you or me but insignificant, indeed, for the gentry.

The primary notable architectural feature of the place was a rather lovely sixteenth-century chapel to St Mary that warranted mention in more discerning guidebooks of the county. The other unusual thing about Henwood House was its isolation, which rather reinforced its lowly status. The nearest habitations to the house were at Henwood Village, and they were down four miles of muddy track. The nearest proper town was Petersfield - the best part of an hour from the house in a fast coach during clement weather. Keeping the place well provisioned must have been quite a chore.

We were met at the door to the house by the butler, a tall, thin fellow in his fifties with a slightly predatory cast to his face. "Gentlemen, Miss Redvers welcomes you. My name is Howard.

The rural Henwood House

Please, do come in." He made a gesture.

"I see you're a left-handed man," Holmes observed. "And a darts player."

"That I am, sir," Howard said, his voice curious.

"The small, callused ridges arising from repeated contact with the grooved shaft of a dart are quite distinctive," Holmes said.

"Intriguing. If you would like to follow me?"

We took the hint and allowed the fellow to lead us to a little parlour with a cosily rustic feel. A young woman rose as we approached, greeted Holmes and me by name, and introduced herself as Gwendoline Redvers.

Miss Gwendoline Redvers

"Thank you so much for coming. Something is very wrong here," she told us once we were seated and past the pleasantries. "I am exceedingly worried for my father. His health is poor, but the cause of the malaise seems beyond the skill of our doctors to diagnose. I came here to care for him a month ago. When he started seeing apparitions out in the grounds, I feared he was losing his mind - until I saw one myself, tall and pale and dreadful. I would have suspected a cruel prank, perhaps, but, as you will have seen, we are isolated here. The whole household was accounted for, and the residents of Henwood are neither young nor spry. The commitment required to travel here and access our grounds at night without drawing notice would itself speak of a frightening level of dedication."

"Quite so," Holmes said. "It is clear to me that someone bears your father considerable malice, and we are here to discover who and why. I assume you do not know of any likely reasons for ill feeling."

She shook her head. "I do not. But we are not a close family. My sister and I are cordial enough and, in fact, she is here at the moment as well. She is my only sibling. Our father was distant when we were children, and after our mother died, he withdrew further from us. I know little of his business, personal or otherwise. If he did accrue enemies, I know nothing of it. I would like to tell you that Father will speak openly with you, but that seems vanishingly unlikely."

The maid, Sylvia

In fact, we did not get to see the father at all that day. Miss Redvers and her sister, Mrs Phoebe Whateley, were perfectly pleasant companions, but we were unable to learn anything more useful. Holmes, to my surprise, was content to bide his time. He hoped to catch a revelatory glimpse of the phantom who, we were told, appeared most nights at around ten p.m. At about four in the afternoon, the butler departed on a visit to a colleague in Petersfield, leaving us in the care of a pair of maids named Sylvia and Millie, the redoubtably stern cook, Mrs Maxwell, and the sisters. Mr Redvers remained in his rooms all evening, although Gwendoline did assure us that he had agreed to at least meet us on the morrow. The phantom did not appear to schedule, and Holmes and I retired around ten thirty.

I was awakened from a sound sleep by a despairing wail. Holmes and I dashed downstairs to investigate and discovered the sisters in considerable distress in their father's rooms. Reminding them that I was, after all, a doctor, I pushed through. Their father was sitting in a chair at the desk in his study, quite dead. He'd been a large man once, but he'd lost considerable weight over the years, and his shrivelled, wrinkled appearance was worst around his lower face, where the skin was somewhat reddened. His hair was sparse - even patchy - and his hands looked weak and liver-spotted. Despite all the indicators of ill health, his expression was peaceful. I shooed the women out and examined the body carefully, but there were no wounds or abrasions, nor even a visible needle mark.

"You realize, I'm sure, that he was murdered," Holmes said, quite unnecessarily, I felt.

How does Holmes know that Redvers was murdered?

The case continues overleaf

THE PHANTOM OF HENWOOD HOUSE

ANSWER on page 214

One of my poor attempts at a self-portrait

THE PHANTOM OF HENWOOD HOUSE

PART TWO

"I, for one, will not miss him."

O nce we had completed our examination of the unfortunate Mr Redvers, we turned our attention to the study that he had been in. Given the marking associated with suffocation, I was looking for a cloth, and I found one quite readily, near the chair in which the victim had died. It looked perfectly ordinary to me, but Holmes took one glance at it and announced that it had come from the house's own linen supplies.

"Do you not see the thread count, my dear fellow? It's identical to that of the tablecloth and napkins we saw last night, as well as the sheets our beds were made up with. There are telltale stitches at the seams on all those pieces that are characteristic of the fabric-makers of Southampton. Given the size, this is certainly another table napkin, possibly even one we have already seen in service. But look, here." He gestured across the room.

The wall of the room was interrupted by a pair of glass-paned doors that looked out onto the lawns at the rear of the house. One of the panes next to the door's handle had been broken, and glass was scattered across the carpet. We walked over for a better look. A flagstone outside the doors provided a step out onto the grass, but there was a clear footprint near the broken pane, with some slivers of glass crunched down into it. It faced the door in exactly the position an intruder might have used to surreptitiously approach the entry prior to forcing entrance.

A footprint, clear as mud

"It looks as if the killer broke in," I said.

Holmes's eyes narrowed slightly. "It would be simple enough to muffle the sound of a small pane of breaking glass with the use of a piece of cloth. Shaking it clean afterward could easily account for the presence of these slivers. The noise would still have alarmed Mr Redvers if he had been in the room, unless he was the heaviest of sleepers, but he could easily have been smothered in his bed and moved to his chair afterward."

It was perhaps six in the morning, and the butler was not expected back from his journey to Petersfield for several more hours. With no coach at the house until his return, and no communications - and no guarantee of either at Henwood Village - there was little we could practically do to alert the outside world. All that remained was to speak to the sisters, the maids and the cook in the hopes that they had heard or seen something useful or could otherwise shed light on the events.

Miss Redvers was, unsurprisingly, in deep distress. "I was too late," she lamented. "I should have contacted you a week ago or more. It's my fault he's dead. If you'd been here sooner, if father had been less stubborn ... " I attempted to ease her from her self-recrimination. "Thank you, doctor. I wish I knew something more that would be of use to you, but I am afraid that I do not. I did not sleep well or soundly but, even so, I did not hear anything odd or suspicious at any point in the night. Phoebe and I retired just a few minutes after you did, but I checked in on Father before I went. He was lying down and feeling crotchety about it, as he had been all day. It is easy enough to imagine that he might have chosen to sit up for a time in the small hours. I bade him a good night. A good night ... " It was clear that she would be able to tell us nothing more and we excused ourselves to give her some privacy.

Phoebe Whateley was pale but well-composed, a few years older than her sister, with the telltale signs of exhaustion common to young mothers. "Father's death is a shocking turn," she told us. "I heard nothing, alas. I half feared the old buzzard would outlive the both of us, you know. He treated our mother horribly. Gwen didn't like to think about it, and even made efforts not to notice his philandering when mother needed our support the most. I don't blame Gwen, and I'm here this weekend to offer her some support, but I can't ever quite forgive her either. I don't know anything about my father's financial affairs, but I can easily imagine a string of enraged fathers, husbands, brothers and even sons reaching out to engulf him. If his business affairs were anything like his romantic ones, enemies would be in plentiful supply. I feel bad for my boys - he was a fond grandfather - but I, for one, will not miss him."

Mrs Phoebe Whateley

After the sisters, we spoke to the staff. The first maid, Millie, was a nervous slip of a thing, with long, tied-up hair and a reflexive stoop that was almost a cower. "I didn't hear or see anything," she told us. "I finished up around midnight and I went straight to my bed, and I didn't hear or see anything." Her voice sounded far less vehement than her repeated words, as if she was on the verge of turning the denial into a question. Holmes looked thoughtful but permitted her to take her leave.

The other maid, Sylvia, was more forthright, if no more helpful. "I'm very sorry, gentlemen. Everything seemed absolutely normal. I completed my work, went to bed and fell straight asleep. Despite what others might say, I never had any problems with Mr Redvers or his daughters. It's not my place to say more, even had there been any more to be said."

Finally, we spoke to the cook, Mrs Maxwell. "I stayed here last night, yes. I don't always, but I do have a room set aside. It's Mr Howard who takes me home of a night and picks me up in the morning, so when he's off, here I am. I'm not a sound sleeper, but I didn't hear anything out of the ordinary in the night. Just the usual creaks and movements. It's clear you gents feel that there's something uncanny going on. Well, Mr Redvers was a bit of a devil in his younger years, but he's been settled down for a decade or more, and if someone decided to finally take revenge, they've waited a good long time for it."

After she'd departed, I looked at

The nervous maid, Millie

Holmes. "That was all of little use," I said.

"Precious little," he agreed. "Old grudges may shed light on a motive, but it told us nothing more."

"So how are we going to find the intruder?"

He sighed. "Watson, do try to pay attention. There was no intruder."

What does Holmes mean?

The case continues overleaf

The Phantom of Henwood House

Answer on page 214

THE PHANTOM OF HENWOOD HOUSE

PART THREE

I had to admit that I had not, in fact, noticed that.

"So where does that leave us?" I asked Holmes. "Are you suggesting that one of these ladies murdered the fellow?"

"It's a possibility," Holmes said. "He was ill and weak, and it would take little force to overpower him, particularly if he was already in bed. So the physical aspect is not an issue. However, my dear Watson, you may have noticed that the depth of the pressure marks on the victim's face display a noticeable extra pressure on the right-hand side."

I had to admit that I had not, in fact, noticed that.

"If the fellow was killed in his chair, from behind, then the pressure on the right side would suggest a right-handed killer. However, I think that, on balance, it is unlikely he was attacked there. I would have expected at least some sound or sign of struggle if he had been awake and in his study, even assuming the window was broken after the murder. Something would surely have been kicked over or moved a little, and this would have left observable traces, even if corrected scrupulously. No, I think he was killed in bed and, if that was the case, the attacker was face to face with him, and the pressure then suggests a left-handed murderer. The only left-handed person in this household is the butler, Howard."

"You think he lied about leaving for Petersfield?"

"We shall learn more when he

An unburdened Millie

returns. In the meantime, we should speak further with Millie and see if she can be persuaded to honesty."

Miss Redvers agreed to send the woman back to us without comment and, a minute later, the young woman re-entered. She looked even more pitiful than last time - if I may speak frankly, she was a quivering mess.

"God is very important to you, is he not?" Holmes asked her, his voice gentle.

Millie was startled into actually looking up at him.

"You have been praying very hard this morning."

She paled and nodded.

With Holmes's question in my mind, I squinted as hard as I could at where her knees would be under her skirts and, indeed, there were some faint suggestions of dust there.

"I know what God has been telling you," Holmes said, his voice transcendent. He didn't have a religious molecule in his body but, at that moment, with that beatific expression on his face, I could have believed that he was the Pope of Rome. "He wants you to tell us the truth. You will be safe. Unburden your soul, child."

She shuddered and started crying. "Yes, sir! Yes!" she managed between sobs. She forced herself to calm a little but the tears did not stop. "I ... I was certain I caught a glimpse of Mr Howard last night as I was heading to bed. He looked so ferocious. He's not a kind man, sir, and I knew he was away. The thought of what he might do if I accused him of something so heinous when he wasn't even in the house ... But I can't lie any more. I may just be a stupid little girl but I truly think I saw him and, if he ... hurts me, at least I'll go with an easy heart."

Holmes nodded in satisfaction and gestured to me to take care of the woman. I put on my gentlest bedside manner and spent some minutes reassuring her that we would keep her perfectly safe, and that she had been invaluably helpful with her bravery. Holmes watched this process with a certain wry amusement.

We left Millie in the care of Miss Redvers and her sister, and asked the other maid, Sylvia, to keep an eye open for the approach of a coach.

A little after half past nine, Sylvia arrived to inform us that she had spotted a coach approaching over the ridge. Some minutes later, the vehicle arrived - driven, as expected, by the butler,

The dreaded coach, approaching

THE PHANTOM OF HENWOOD HOUSE

Howard. Holmes and I were outside to meet him. My trusty Webley revolver was near to hand.

Howard pulled up, looking at us curiously, and got down from the coach. "Gentlemen? Is something the matter?" He seemed perfectly relaxed, although he was clearly quite exhausted.

Holmes watched him calmly. "Your employer, Mr Redvers, has died."

"That's terrible," Howard said, without much conviction or surprise. "I should turn the horses around and fetch the coroner."

"Or the police," I muttered.

"Oh?" Howard looked a little surprised. "You suspect foul play?"

"Where were you last night, Mr Howard?" Holmes asked.

The fellow actually smiled. "Uppark House at South Harting, a few miles on the other side of Petersfield. Miss Featherstonehaugh regularly holds large dinners for her friends, often with dancing in

Howard, ready with an extensive alibi

the grand ballroom. Her head butler, Peter Bayliss, is a good friend of mine and, on particularly important events, I go over to help him out with the organization. I was there by six. Miss Featherstonehaugh had a pair of admirals amongst the guests last night, along with an archbishop, two peers and a cousin of the Duke of Cornwall. Poor Bayliss needed all the steady hands he could get. I was on duty providing assistance to the guests until some time after three in the morning, and back on again at five to help with the breakfast rush. It was exhausting, but very rewarding." He paused for a long moment, savouring the situation. "There's no way I know of to get from Uppark to Henwood and back in two hours, and I distinctly remember helping Admiral Penn find a deck of playing cards at ten to three in the morning. He'd taken quite the liking to me early in the evening and had kept me close at hand whenever possible." Another pause. "I find I have that effect on people of character."

"I see," Holmes said.

"I fear that if you have been suspecting me of evil plots and dark deeds, you have been significantly misled. Whatever did or did not happen here last night, it's quite impossible that I was involved."

"Not impossible at all, in fact," Holmes replied. "Merely unlikely. Watson, please cover Mr Howard with your revolver whilst I restrain him."

How does Holmes think the butler did it?

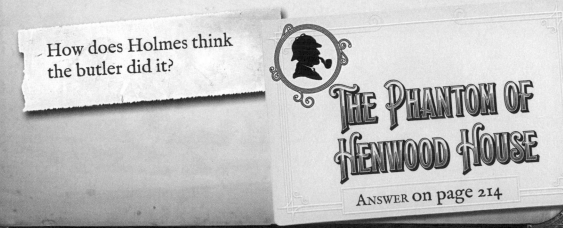

THE PHANTOM OF HENWOOD HOUSE

ANSWER on page 214

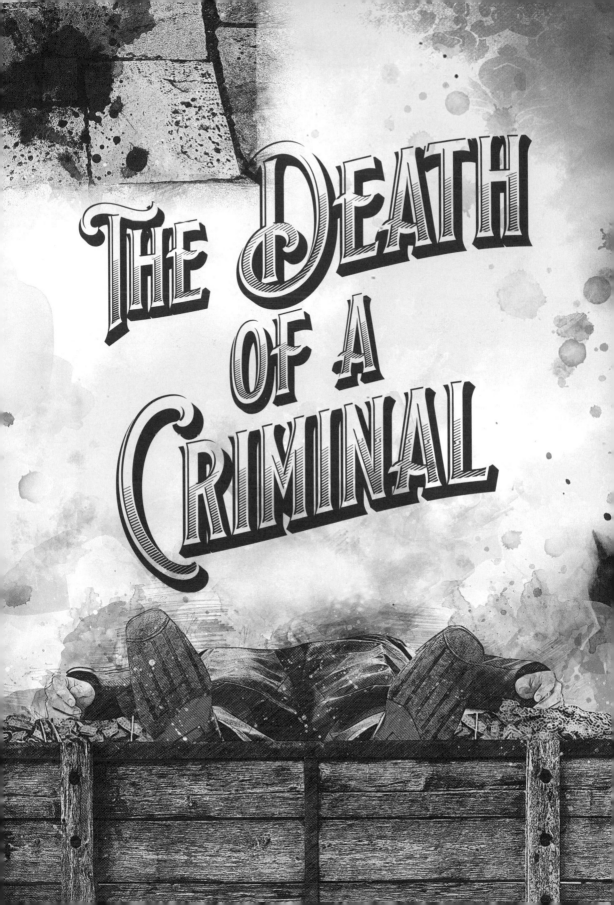

THE DEATH
OF A CRIMINAL

PART ONE

"Fletcher had been stabbed through the heart - one
neat blow by the looks of it."

It was a week or so before Christmas and Lestrade had brought Holmes an early gift: an extended Monday-morning session of pleading, cajoling, wheedling and appeals to better nature. He had, of course, been handed a case that had stymied him from the outset, along with an extra helping of pressure and expectation. Holmes was engaged in a series of chemical experiments upon a bewildering array of petals from all manner of flowers and had little interest in playing the inspector's "pet crime monkey", as he put it. However, Lestrade is nothing if not persistent and, over the years, he has learnt some tricks of his own when it comes to the management of my friend. Eventually, Holmes agreed in bad humour to assist, if for no other reason than to shut the fellow up.

A Barings executive banker, one Bertie Fletcher, had been found dead in a large rubbish skip near the river, a little to the west of Tower Bridge. He had been with the merchant bank for 20 years or more, and was a well-respected member of the City's financial community, with the power and connections that entailed. The location of his corpse particularly unsettled Barings, suggesting as it did some scandalous entanglement with criminal elements. They were extremely keen to get the matter handled as swiftly and quietly as

Lestrade is nothing if not persistent

possible. Whilst they stopped short of actually demanding that any impropriety on Fletcher's part be left uncovered, they certainly made their preferences in that direction quite plain.

Holmes, of course, was in no mood to pander to a bank, and his first questions to Lestrade were regarding the character of the deceased. The inspector was all too aware of his tenuous hold on Holmes's cooperation. "I've spoken to a few people this morning," he confessed. "Assistants and the like, before the board sent out word that shut them all up tighter than a safe door. Several mentioned a whiff of scandal about the man, but nobody would admit to knowing anything directly. One said a friend mentioned hearing of 'questionable tastes in entertainment', another that a cousin had been to the man's home and seen a finer collection of art than would have been expected. That sort of thing. Nothing we can act on. Now, please, can I take you to the scene?"

Holmes grudgingly agreed, and we bundled up and went forth into the December cold. When we got to the site, the river was unusually high, almost up to its banks. It is easy to forget that the Thames is a force of nature, until one sees it lashing angrily at its embankments. The skip that Fletcher had been found in was at the entrance to an alley running back from the river, guarded by a stolid-looking constable.

"I managed to keep the body in place for now," Lestrade said. "I can't hold on tmuch longer. Them on high want it taken in."

Holmes nodded, and he and I went over to the skip to examine it. It was mostly filled with builder's rubble, and the body had been casually tossed on top of that. Fletcher had been stabbed through the heart - one neat blow by the looks of it. His hands, neck and face were unmarked, which suggested that he had

*An inauspicious
resting place*

either been taken by surprise or had been restrained effectively before he'd had a chance to lash out. He'd been dead since Saturday afternoon, by my estimation.

Sherlock, meanwhile, was peering at the man's feet. "He was in Billingsgate Fish Market shortly before his death," he declared. "There are fish scales on the ends of his trousers, and bits of straw slightly higher up, but the clincher is the dust to the left side of the knee here. Its dark colour is quite distinctive and arises from the state of the soil in the market ground. We should uncover the precise location where he was killed."

"I can answer that for you," Lestrade said. "He was dragged down the alley from a disused store room a little further up."

I looked up from the skip and saw a clear swathe trailing through the grime of the alley. Holmes made a quietly non-committal noise but allowed the inspector to lead us up the alley, following the trail to a weathered door. He opened it and we followed him into a fairly small stone-flagstoned storeroom. It gave the impression of having been disused for some time. The floor was mostly clean of dust, but the heavy shutters covering the windows were thick with it, and there were patches of lichen here and there on the old flagstones.

Although someone had clearly swept the floor, there was a thick stain of dried blood in the middle of the room. Lestrade went over to it. "Here you are, Mr Holmes."

"He wasn't killed there, Lestrade," Holmes said. "Surely even you can see that?"

The crime scene?

Why does Holmes think that Fletcher was killed elsewhere?

The case continues opposite

THE DEATH OF A CRIMINAL

ANSWER on page 215

THE DEATH
OF A CRIMINAL

PART TWO

"The ingrained stench of fish guts

hung heavily in the air."

Holmes fixed Lestrade with a steely gaze. "I trust you and your men can uncover the real location of this man's death without my active assistance? Charming as your company always is, there are a number of precipitates that I would very much like to check on. Have a man take Watson and me back to Baker Street. You can return for us once the site is found."

"Mr Holmes, I must stress again that this case is significantly sensitive and must be handled with all possible speed."

"Honestly, man. You hardly need me to examine paperwork for you. If the killer used this particular storage, he must have known it would be safe to do so. Examine the ownership of the unit and the institutions or individuals behind it, and look for similar patterns in the area around Billingsgate. See, also, if there are spaces held notionally empty or unused despite their location, or stretches of alley in the area that are rarely trafficked. This is the most trivial sort of procedure, and I refuse to believe that you and your fellows are too addled to take care of it yourselves.

The business of Billingsgate

You are allowing your worry to cloud your judgement, sir. I am not a safety blanket for you to trail around for comfort."

"I—" Lestrade began.

"I have actually important work to be doing, Lestrade. Take us home and return for us once you have the murder site."

"Yes, Mr Holmes," the inspector managed.

So it was that we were back home and in the warm by eleven

a.m., and Holmes was able to get back to his floral studies. Mrs Hudson provided us with a pleasant lunch of sausages, relish and toast, and I was contemplating picking up a novel at around three p.m. when the inspector's man returned. Holmes shook his head a little but refrained from further grumbling at having to leave his test tubes. I got the feeling that his experiments had proven useful to him, but I forbore from inquiry.

Duty calls

Maybe twenty minutes later, we were being delivered to a road a short distance away from Billingsgate Fish Market. Fortunately, the market had mostly concluded its business by the afternoon but, even so, the ingrained stench of fish guts hung heavily in the air. Lestrade was waiting for us near another storeroom: a significantly larger one than the former. He looked cold and tired and I felt a pang of sympathy for the ratty fellow, but only a small one - I would still rather have been in my armchair with a book and a pipe.

"It was as you said, Mr Holmes," the inspector declared. "There's a different limited company holding this place to the one holding the previous, but they're both held in trust by the same legal firm, and this unit is listed as unused for all that it's right next to the market. I've had a look inside and ... well, you'll see for yourself. But it's the place."

"Good stuff," Holmes said cheerfully. "I knew you had it in you."

We went into the warehouse. Despite its official designation, this one was far from empty. There were several tall rows of crates in sizes ranging from not much larger than a rugby ball to taller and wider than I was. Straw covered much of the floor, but there was an unpleasant smell to the place that carried, despite the heavy air from the fish market - sour sweat, caked-in grime, human waste, rotten blood. In fact, it smelt like some of the worse prisons I've been unfortunate enough to have visited.

Whilst I was puzzling out the air, Holmes was roaming around the room, examining this and that, poking at things, and so on. After a couple of minutes, he went to a place a few feet from the door we'd entered by, and waved to Lestrade and me. "Come, gentlemen."

We obediently joined him and he scuffed at the straw with his foot to expose some stained wood. "This is the precise location of the murder," he said. "The bloodstain is of the right age, and sufficiently extensive for a stab to the heart. Some efforts have been made to scrub it clean but the wood held on to the

The warehouse was far from empty

The crime scene revealed

stain jealously. It is far from the only blood mark in here, but it is the most recent." He turned and pointed to another spot he'd uncovered: a bloody outline of a size-five shoe in a standard-looking cut, heading toward the door. "From the crispness of that print, the blood was still fresh. The killer didn't want to stay around, so he left his fellows to the cleaning up. That suggests a degree of structure to the criminal operation."

"You're sure this storage is used for illicit purposes?" Lestrade asked. "There are plenty of genuine reasons for leaving a place unlisted."

"Have a look around," Holmes said. "Along that wall over there, you'll find crates of sailor's rations, mostly empty. There are a number of barrels of water nearby, also partly used. Who stores such things? Note, then, that several of the empty crates are suspiciously large, with plenty of straw, and evidence of staining. There are no large pieces of statuary in evidence that would require such a huge box, and statues leave no stench. There are rare pigments, expensive liqueurs, religious icons, chinaware and other commonly smuggled goods here, yes. But the real cargo is human." He'd been walking across the room as he spoke and now he pulled aside a sheet of tarp that was covering a big pile of boxes. Behind it, to my astonishment, was a long, low cell made of bars. "Fletcher was killed by slavers and, from the fact of his being here, it is likely he was involved."

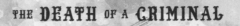

*The most foul
sort of cell*

Lestrade looked deeply dismayed. "That's horrible, of course, but it's not exactly a definitive solution. There's a couple of dozen flesh-traders that we know of in the city but haven't yet been able to string up."

I couldn't help myself. "A couple of dozen? Slavery's been outlawed for fifty years!"

"That's not so long, my dear fellow," Holmes said. "Old habits die hard, and old sources of profit die harder still. Slavery is entrenched, and not just in the brothels. It is disgusting, but then so is much of human nature. And Lestrade, you're not thinking clearly. You can rule out the lion's share of those villains, I'm sure."

What does Holmes mean?

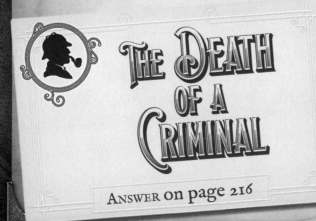

THE **DEATH** OF A **CRIMINAL**

*The case continues
opposite*

THE DEATH OF A CRIMINAL

PART THREE

"It would have been easy to overlook the gleam of cunning intelligence in his eyes."

Before we left, Lestrade assured us that he would round up all the possible candidates that Scotland Yard knew of, and Holmes agreed to question them once they'd been assembled. The next afternoon, Lestrade's man conveyed us to a police station in the City, just a short distance from Liverpool Street station. We were met by the inspector and shown to a pleasant interview room.

"I've got three for you, Holmes," he said. "We don't have any solid proof that any of them are dirty, or we'd have already arrested them. I'm not even completely certain that they all are. But word is persistent, and they have the attribute you wanted."

"What have you told them?" he asked.

"That we found an influential banker dead early on Monday morning and we are canvassing all manner of important folks to try to discover if anyone knew anything of his activities or contacts. We're running it soft and gentle. That won't have washed with them. They're canny enough to know we're fishing for someone to charge. They're all playing along as if they believe that we believe what we're saying so far, though."

He passed Holmes some files on the three individuals and left to send the first person in.

Alfred Dayson was a short, muscular man in his late forties with a perpetual sneer and a brutish face. It would have been easy to overlook the gleam of cunning intelligence in his eyes. According to Lestrade's notes, he ran a vicious criminal gang and had a reputation for sadism. The gang dealt in all manner of illicit activity, from the typical burglary, mugging and extortion, to gambling, prostitution and even occasional murder-for-hire. Dayson was careful to keep his own nose clean, though, and had his men so terrorized that none ever spoke against him.

Alfred Dayson

"I ain't never heard of this Mr Fletcher of yours," he declared. "I certainly wasn't nowhere near the fish market any time recently. I had a busy weekend, in fact, between the family and the business. South of the river the entire time. Haven't had so much as a minute to myself since Wednesday last, and there's plenty who'll confirm the truth of that. Besides, I ain't got no time for bankers and fancy folk. I'm a working man, ain't I. Honest day's pay for an honest day's work. That's enough for me. My work? A bit of buying, a bit of selling, whatever comes my way. Me and the lads have a knack for finding the right bloke at the right time. But bankers and that, that's a bit rich for my blood. Trouble, that sort are. Demanding. I'm not much of a one for heeding demands."

The next file introduced Helena Kenzie, a sculptor of modest fame and, according to Lestrade's notes, a smuggler of artworks of various sorts who always managed to stay one step ahead of his efforts. He also noted that repeated information pegged her as the madam of a network of high-end brothels across London, which she ran through sufficient blinds and proxies as to ensure the absence of any actual evidence. She proved to be a refined, pleasant and quite lovely woman of perhaps thirty, dressed in elegant but not ostentatious clothes.

Helena Kenzie, sculptor and smuggler

"I'm afraid that I do not immediately recall knowing a Bertie Fletcher," she told us. Her voice was light and highly educated. "It's possible that we have met, however. I attend quite a lot of social functions. It's very important if one is to be successful as an artist. I'm lucky in that I like company, which is not always true of my peers. It can be a lonely business, creating art, and many of the people it attracts are perfectly self-sufficient in that regard. I prefer to get out and about when I'm not working. I spent Saturday in Bromley, for example. I was there by eleven, setting up for a rather well-received exhibition that evening. You can read a little about it in yesterday's *Standard*."

Morgan Harbison, antiquities dealer and smuggler

The third person was a polite, slender man in his forties named Morgan Harbison. He was a dealer in antiquities and curiosities in his public life, and an efficient, cautious and quite unprovable smuggler of a broad range of goods, if Lestrade's information was accurate.

"I believe I met the fellow once or twice," he said. "He was a collector of some sort, yes? I didn't do any business with him that I recall. I tend to remember clients a little more clearly than I do prospects. I certainly didn't know him well enough to have any idea of his movements, and I haven't been anywhere near Billingsgate in weeks. As a matter of fact, I was in Oxford from Friday through to Monday evening as the guest of the Dean of St John's College. He's a delightful fellow and very enthusiastic about Anglo-Saxon artefacts. I have some pieces coming in from a French collection later in the week, including a particularly fine brooch that he is enthused to see."

Once he had departed, Holmes permitted himself a brief smile. "That went quite well, old friend."

"It did?" I asked. "Seemed like a load of old flannel to me."

"Any scrap of cloth can offer revelations," Holmes said. "You did not identify the killer then?"

Who does Holmes think the murderer is?

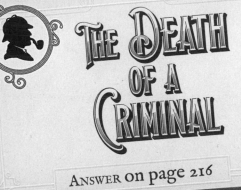

THE DEATH OF A CRIMINAL

ANSWER on page 216

Wapping Docks

THE PHANTOM

PART ONE

"I do not believe in phantoms, and I do not believe that the police are seriously attempting to find Simon's murderer."

Paul Brannon was an engineer and, by the cut of his clothes, a reasonably successful one at that. He was a tall man, handsome in an understated way, and approaching forty years old, judging by the lines around his eyes and the hints of grey in his hair. He was currently sitting in one of the armchairs in the living room of 221b.

"My cousin Simon is an architect," he told us. "Was," he amended. "He was found murdered out at Wapping Docks three nights ago. The police have not, as yet, apprehended any suspects. In fact, the sergeant handling the death told me yesterday that they were 'looking for a phantom'. I can't say with any certainty whether he was speaking figuratively or literally but, in either case, I do not believe in phantoms, and I do not believe that the police are seriously attempting to find Simon's murderer."

"Why was your cousin out at the docks?" Holmes asked.

"I haven't got the faintest idea," Brannon said. "We have collaborated on a couple of building projects, but we are not colleagues. Simon was part of a reasonably large architectural firm, one which undoubtedly has plenty of junior staff suitable to act as dogsbodies and do things like visit dockyards. As for personal reasons, again, I can think of nothing that would have dragged him out to such a place. He was a quiet man, funny and wry, and he preferred his books and diagrams to ... well, pretty much everything else."

Holmes frowned thoughtfully. "A murderous phantom. Well. We will look into the matter for you. I would like to know why a policeman would use such a curious word."

So it was that, shortly before lunchtime, we found ourselves arriving at Scotland Yard to speak to one Sergeant Daniel

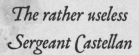

*The rather useless
Sergeant Castellan*

Castellan regarding the murder. Holmes and I are well known at the reception of the Yard, and we were swiftly shown to a waiting room. And wait we did.

It took Sergeant Castellan a solid forty minutes to make the time to speak to us. When he arrived, he turned out to be a beefy, slovenly man with small eyes and a discouragingly thuggish expression. "What?" he demanded by way of introduction.

Holmes glanced at him coolly. "I see you've beaten your wife so savagely that she's been unable to do anything around the house for the last two days."

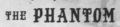

"How dare—" began the sergeant, swelling up.

Holmes crossed the room swiftly to stand no more than an inch from the man's nose, his face a mask of disdain. "Bruised knuckles. Scruffy shoes. Unpressed trousers. A stain of some cheap source on your collar. A wedding ring, dull and dented but present. You are a coward and a thug, and I pity the poor woman who has to tolerate your continued failure as a human being. Do you imagine any of your superiors would stand against Detective Inspector Lestrade if I insisted he facilitate your dismissal as a condition of working with him in the future? Or would they be glad to be rid of a violent fool promoted above his station?"

The man shuddered, fear, rage and humiliation fighting on his face. Rage lost, and he took a step back from Holmes.

"Better," Holmes said. "I am going to have your wife watched closely, sergeant. I cannot abide a man who takes his resentments out on the helpless. The next time she sports so much as a bruise, the axe will fall. And I do mean that quite literally."

"What do you want from me?" the sergeant whined. "Sirs."

"The murder of Simon Brannon. Tell me about it."

The resentment slammed back into his voice. "It's a bloody fool's errand, I'll tell you that much. We found the body in an alley next to the Wandering Bishops pub. He'd been sliced from neck to navel, guts spilling out. Savage piece of knife work. The landlord of the pub spoke to the bl— uh, the victim before he died. Says the man staggered into his pub as he was closing up, grabbed him urgently and led him outside. Pointed across the dock to where a man was watching them - a beanpole of a man, six feet or so with wild, bushy white hair, no beard, and a scar down one cheek. The victim managed to get out the word 'Baker'. Then he died, and this Baker fellow turned and scarpered. The landlord was terrified. We've been canvassing the docks and the ships for two days. There's no sign of the man. He's gone, I tell you. Jumped back on a ship and sailed off to Christ knows where."

"Nonsense," Holmes snapped.

Why does Holmes doubt the sergeant's account?

THE PHANTOM

The case continues opposite

ANSWER on page 217

THE PHANTOM

PART TWO

"Tall bastards, they were, and far too free with the
singing. Good drinkers, though."

Holmes glared down at Sergeant Castellan. "I see that there is nothing of any use to be had here. Come, Watson. We have better things to do than this. Remember, sergeant, I have eyes everywhere, and they will be watching. Pray you do not come to my attention again." He swept past the horrified and enraged policeman, and I followed. I'm not sure if the man heeded Holmes's warning but, either way, my old friend never mentioned him to me again.

We caught a cab to Wapping Docks, which let us out a short walk from the Wandering Bishops. The area was busy and ripe with the inevitable smells of seafaring commerce. It was, at least, not a dock for fishing vessels, so the stench was less potent than it might have been. We made our way down the street to the pub, which distinguished itself with a sign of several exalted clergymen walking nervously down a thickly forested path.

Holmes noticed my curiosity. "It's a common enough pub name in Hookland. There was an incident on Barrowcross Moor last century. They found one of the bishops in the end, but he was quite mad."

"I see," I said.

We went in. To my surprise, the place was perfectly pleasant. The furniture was on the cheap side, and the decor tended to the nautical - scraps of sail and netting, oars, ship's wheels and such - but it was far cleaner and brighter than I had expected. There were a dozen or so men in the bar, and it was less than a third full. A tall chap was behind the counter, slim and well kept, with a shock of greying curls atop his head and a pair of wired spectacles.

We crossed over to him.

"Are you the landlord, sir?" Holmes asked.

The cab to Wapping Docks

"Greg Proutt at your service," the fellow replied. "What will it be?"

"My name is Sherlock Holmes and this is my companion, Dr Watson. We're investigating the murder of Simon Brannon three nights ago."

"With the police are you, sirs?"

Holmes frowned. "I have spoken with the idiot the police have assigned to this case and I assure you that I am in no way interested in the nonsense you told him."

Proutt's expression lightened. "Thank God for that. That stupid sergeant kept insisting I knew something and slapped me around until I made up some horseshit to get rid of him. Then he swallowed the lot like it was nectar."

"I suspected as much," Holmes said. "I take it you saw nothing?"

"Not a thing. But a couple of my regulars did, I learned the next day. Fred and Dick." He pointed to a table across the pub, not far from the dartboard. "They're right there. They'll happily tell you all about it in exchange for a scotch each."

Holmes arched an eyebrow, but bought the drinks, and we carried them over. The pair looked up as we approached, curious but not hostile. Holmes set the drinks down in front of them and said, in a surprisingly coarse, London-accented voice, "Greg said as you lads might be happy to tell me a story in return for a little whistle-wetter. I'm Holmes, this is Watson."

"Fred Jackson," said the older of the men. "And this is Dick Keefe. Very neighbourly of you. Pull up a chair."

We sat down and I let Holmes exchange pleasantries with the men. After a short while, he steered the conversation round to the murder, and how bereft the victim's cousin was.

"We saw him, all right," Fred said. He was a lugubrious man with a face rather like a basset hound, and a faint odour of resin. "Didn't know what he was about at the time, mind. Very tall, that was what stuck out. At least six foot six, and most of it was in his legs. It was dark - so I didn't see much of his face - only that he was pale-skinned. He'd stick out in a crowd, though, that's for sure. He stalked off toward the warehouses."

"It was Clarence's warehouse," said Dick. He was a young man, but looked older, with a face that suggested a stint as a boxer. However, he had kindly eyes. "I was over the other side of the wharf, see. I didn't see where he come from, but I spotted him stalking across the way like some sort of spider, all gangly, like. He went into Harper's - that's the warehouse Clarence

THE **PHANTOM**

Fred Jackson and Dick Keefe

manages. Then I spotted Fred and went over to him, and we decided to drop in here to have a quick one for the road. The dead man was huddled in the mouth of the alley. I might not have noticed, except for the stink of fresh death." He shook his head. "Horrible. We called for a bobby and then got out of there. There's no sense sticking around. Didn't mean for Greg to get slapped about. I'd have stayed if I'd known the coppers would get handsy."

"Either of you seen hide or hair of this tall man since?" Holmes asked.

"Not a sausage," Fred said. "Not had anyone that tall here since the last time a crew of Norwegians came in, what, six weeks ago?"

"Seven," Dick said. "Yeah. Tall bastards, they were, and far too free with the singing. Good drinkers, though, and convivial company."

"Right you are," Holmes said. "Thanks, lads. You've been a great help. I'll leave another behind the bar for you."

They gave us a cheery wave as we departed. Holmes left a whole shilling with the barman and we left the pub. I rather regretted not asking for a pickled egg before we left, but that was by the by.

"You believe them?" I asked.

Holmes nodded. "They were telling us the truth." He reached over to pluck off a piece of straw that I'd failed to notice attach itself to my lapel.

"Well, a man that tall should be fairly easy to find, at least."

"Don't be so sure, old friend," Holmes replied.

What does Holmes mean?

The case continues overleaf

THE PHANTOM

ANSWER on page 217

THE PHANTOM

PART THREE

"No, we do not keep a log. That's, ah, not a popular precaution."

Harper's Warehouse was easily distinguished, thanks to the name painted on the side of the building. It was only an ambitious stone's throw from the Wandering Bishops. Inside, we found a tidy and well-organized space with extensive shelving, as well as open areas for larger crates and packages. About half of the space was used. There were a couple of men near the entrance, and one of them readily went to fetch the manager, whose full name, we learned, was Clarence Winson.

A minute or two later, Winson appeared. He was an unobtrusive man - medium height and build, harmless appearance, inoffensively decent clothing. He'd have made a perfect pickpocket. When he spoke, however, his voice was deep and rich. "Good afternoon, gentlemen. How may I be of service?"

Holmes and I led him a short way away from the other men and explained that we were investigating a death and wanted to speak to a man who'd been seen entering the warehouse late at night a few days ago.

"Tides are impatient, as I'm sure you know, and I have to make sure that the warehouse is accessible at all hours. With that said, entry is restricted to current clients between eight p.m. and five a.m. I keep a night watchman on duty to ensure that there are no intruders. If your witness is correct, that would suggest that he saw one of the keyholders. Three days ago,

Clarence Winson

123

we had four gentlemen on the books. One sailed for Biscay yesterday, but the other three are still here, in nearby boarding houses."

"Do you have records of who came in and when?"

"No, we do not keep a log. That's, ah, not a popular precaution."

"I see," Holmes said. "Could you give me the names of the men who are still here?"

Winson looked uncomfortable. "I understand that you're trying to solve a crime, but my clients do value their privacy."

Holmes fished in his pocket and then held out a goodly amount of coins.

"I ... " Winson took the handout. "I can make an exception this once, I suppose. It is for a good cause."

Five minutes later, we had the names of the three men and the ships they represented. It turned out to be easy to get to speak to them, which should not have surprised me, given that they were merchants. Holmes announced we would approach them in that regard and see what could be learned obliquely.

Captain Theodore Adamson of *Ganymede* was a tall man in his thirties, about six feet or so, with sandy hair and a close-trimmed beard and moustache. He had a habit of twitching his head slightly at random intervals. "We've got a selection of the finest cheeses from across France, gents," he

*Information is not
always cheap*

Captain Theodore Adamson

told us. "All carefully preserved in tight barrels. Very popular with the restaurants around town, they are. Go down a treat with the upper classes too. Very exclusive. Well, yes, I could do a run to Dublin for you, of course. *Ganymede*'s a barque so she's not the fastest thing out there but, even with the extra day or two, I can still come in cheaper than anyone else around here. She has a net registered tonnage of two hundred and thirty."

Captain Douglas Nicholson of *Restoration* was somewhat older-looking than Captain Adamson, but similarly tall, and missing the tip of the little finger on his left hand. "Right now, I've got a hold full of luxury goods out of Holland. Fine Delftware - complete sets - along with spices from the Far East, particularly cinnamon and nutmeg, and several boxes of pure, powdered cocoa. You could make a household or six very happy with my wares, gents. I suppose we could head to Ireland for you, once this lot is accounted for. *Restoration*

Denis Hughes

is a schooner, so it's fast and we don't have to worry overmuch about facing winds. If you're concerned about perishables, there's no need."

The third man, Denis Hughes, was the first mate of *The Gurkha*, a brig out of Southampton, and looked perfectly normal, although he, too, was about six feet in height. "We're just back from Porto. Five hundred casks of the finest aged port you'll see this side of a gentleman's club. And that's just what we've got left. It's been a busy few days. If you want to take some off my hands, you'll have to move sharpish because I'm expecting two more callers today alone. It's not cheap but it's damned fine. Ireland? Not immediately, I'm afraid. Captain's heading to Copenhagen in a few days with a cargo of worsted. After that, though, perhaps. *The Gurkha*'s a fast lady when she puts her mind to it. We could be there by the middle of next month, I'm sure. Maybe a couple of days later if we can find a cargo from Denmark to Ireland, but that would cut your costs in half."

Five minutes later, we were back in the Wandering Bishops for a warming ale and a snack to eat. Holmes seemed in an oddly good mood, given the tedious flannel we'd sat through.

"I didn't realize you were so interested in commerce," I told him.

He scoffed. "Those pirates? Hardly. I really did think you'd have spotted the murderer, old friend."

Who does Holmes think the killer is?

THE PHANTOM

ANSWER on page 217

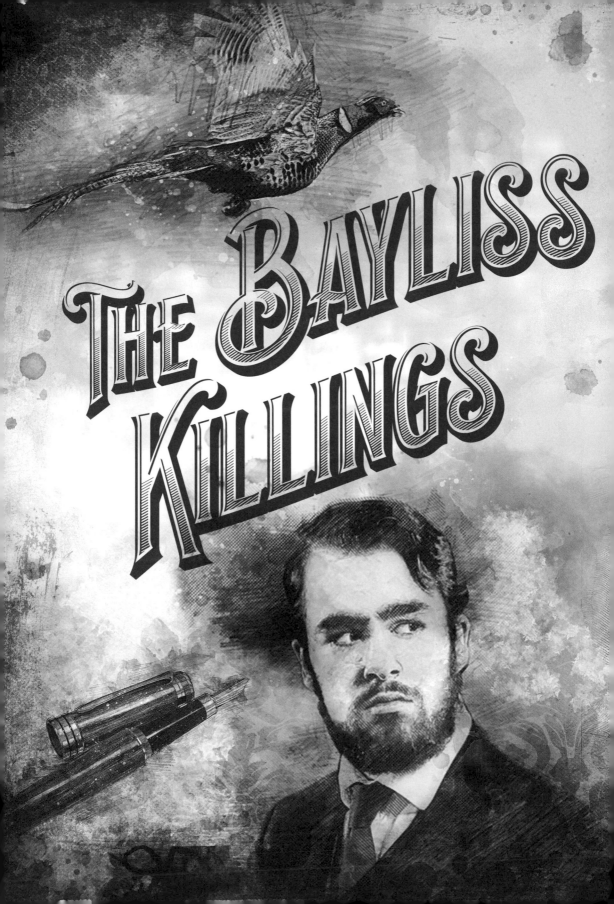

THE BAYLISS KILLINGS

PART ONE

"Mr Bayliss! Please, control yourself.

Remember your breeding, sir!"

It was early January, and the weather outside was tempestuous. In this, it mirrored somewhat the situation inside our rooms at 221b - not because of any tension between Holmes and myself, but because of the presence of an unusually stormy client. Wilfred Bayliss was a tall, thin man with all the hallmarks of a habitual worrywart. He had arrived in a state of significant excitation and, from there, had worked himself up into a frenzy. As I understood his rantings, his father and then his brother had been murdered, and he was terrified that he was to be next.

Holmes was, apparently, somewhat interested in the particulars, as he had not yet thrown the fellow out on his ear, but it was obvious to me that he was losing patience with the

The late
Mr Bayliss

My sternest expression

situation. So, when Bayliss paused to draw breath, I put on the stern face that I use for difficult patients and stepped up close to the man's face. "Mr Bayliss! Please, control yourself," I snapped. "Remember your breeding, sir!" He'd mentioned his father's wealth, so it was a certainty that he'd been schooled in self-control. Bayliss reared back from me, astonished, and I softened my face into my neutral, professionally concerned expression. "Take a deep breath, sir, and release it slowly over the count of five. Then breathe in and out to that measure four more times."

He obeyed me and, over the space of half a minute, the panic in his eyes softened back into mere fear. "Thank you, doctor. My sincere apologies, gentlemen. I will endeavour to remain coherent."

Holmes shot me an appreciative look, then nodded. "Quite. From what you have said so far, I understand that your father has been assassinated, and your elder brother is now, likewise, dead. The details are lacking, however. What more can you tell me?"

Bayliss made a visible effort to steel himself. "My father was Augustus Bryson Bayliss. He founded a textile business in his early twenties with my grandfather's assistance and, over the course of forty years, built it into a very successful enterprise with clients across the continent. When he retired, the firm was selling more than two million items of inventory a year. He undoubtedly made enemies in the course of his professional life but, to the best of my knowledge, at least, he was no more cut-throat or exploitative than any other leading member of the business."

"You did not join the firm, and instead went into logistics," Holmes observed.

Bayliss looked at him curiously. "That's so, but how—?"

"Your coach-wheel cufflinks clearly demonstrate that you are interested in transportation, the style in which you lace your shoes is quite distinctive and most commonly found amongst hauliers, and the pen you keep in your top pocket is unusually sturdy, whilst still remaining decorative - a pen that only a heavy user would ever think to purchase, sir. Your profession is quite plain."

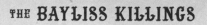

An unusually sturdy fountain pen

The man nodded. "It sounds so simple put like that, but few would think to connect such trivia together. I salute your observational skills, sir."

Hunting pheasant
in the woods

"That is, after all, why you have come to me," Holmes observed, but I could see the small, pleased smile playing across his lips.

"Quite so," Bayliss said thoughtfully. His mania had receded in the face of his intellectual engagement. "So ... I went into logistics to provide my father's firm with the sort of reliable service that it could not seem to obtain through third parties. He provided the initial finance, in the same way his father had helped him. In the last fifteen years, my company has thrived, and we now assist well over two dozen clients. Father's firm has always received the greatest possible care, of course, but I am scrupulous not to short-change others. In the meantime, my brothers Jack and Frederic took positions with the family firm. Frederic, frankly, is not cut out for the world of business, and I understand he has barely ever even bothered attending work. Jack genuinely tried his best but, since Father retired, the firm has been losing ground under his guidance. Which brings us to the last week." He paused and Holmes nodded encouragingly.

"On Saturday, Father was out hunting pheasant in the woods. Mid afternoon, one of the beaters came running back to inform the household that he'd been murdered. The police responded quickly. He'd been shot in the chest with a shotgun and killed instantly. None of the men had seen anything suspicious, and the police found no weapon, shells or useful traces. We all gathered on Sunday and I was in the lounge with Freddy when there was a loud report. I rushed into the dining room to find that Jack had been shot at by some rough-looking cove who'd run off. Fortunately, he missed. Poor Mother had to be sedated and, as you have seen, I am in little better a state myself. Then, on Tuesday morning, the police contacted me again. Jack had been killed. He was, they said, overpowered in his apartment. His throat was cut and he was left on the floor to … bleed out. There were more than six pints of blood."

Jack, throat cut in his apartment?

I did some quick mental mathematics. "He was something over ten stone?" I asked.

"Eleven or so, yes," Bayliss said.

I nodded. "That is certainly consistent with the amount of blood you're describing."

"The police say that once he'd, um, drained sufficiently, the killer wrapped his body in the bedroom rug and dragged it off. They lost track of the trail outside the building. It was put into a coach, they think. The apartment had also been robbed, with several small but expensive trinkets having gone missing. Last night, at least, passed without incident, but I have no idea why this vengeance is being visited upon us. I'm terrified that Freddy or I are next. Which is why I need your help." He swallowed. "Please help."

"We shall," Holmes said. "But let us not assume that your brother is dead."

Bayliss and I both stared at him.

Why does Holmes have doubts that Jack has been murdered?

The case continues opposite

THE BAYLISS KILLINGS

ANSWER on page 218

THE BAYLISS KILLINGS

PART TWO

"One does not consult the foremost expert and
then disagree with his assessments."

After a moment of clearly visible struggle, Wilfred Bayliss
nodded. "I do see your point, sir. I suppose we cannot
be certain of the exact events that occurred at Jack's
apartment. I fail to see other plausible explanations, but I shall
endeavour to retain a degree of hope as to his fate."

"It is often the case that the unlikely proves to be most
enlightening," Holmes said. "I find it serves me best to
assume nothing, and deal, so much as it is possible, only in the
absolutely rigour of fact and observation."

Bayliss nodded again. "Would you like to see the apartment,
then?"

"It may prove useful," Holmes said. "But it is not my first
destination."

I blinked at that. "It isn't?"

Ragged would-be assasin

"We should visit the family home, my dear Watson. I find myself curious regarding this ragged would-be assassin who shot at Mr Bayliss's brother and missed."

"Of course," Bayliss said. He was clearly confused, and I could see the panic stirring within him, waiting for the opportunity to rise once more. "Would you like to visit immediately? We can be there by nightfall."

Holmes shook his head. "Daylight would be more useful. I truly do not believe that any ills will befall your remaining family members at this point but, if you have concerns, I recommend taking a room in a hotel in town for tonight. Perhaps your brother and mother could do the same. That way, it would be quite impossible for any assassin to approach you, particularly one dressed in poor clothing."

Bayliss opened his mouth, his brow creased, and then he closed it again and shook his head in resignation. "As you say, sir. I will trust your judgement. One does not consult the foremost expert and then disagree with his assessments."

"I appreciate your faith, sir," Holmes said. "It is not misplaced, I assure you."

After a little more discussion, we set a time to meet on the morrow at the family home in northern Kent, and Bayliss left. Before he departed, however, I took the opportunity to warn him against laudanum unless absolutely vital, and gave him a small bottle of tincture of hemp, with instructions to use a dropper's worth under his tongue any time he felt he needed medical assistance to help calm his nerves. It is one of the few reasonably effective calmatives that is neither habit-forming nor prone to inducing mania.

The next morning, we took the train out of Charing Cross to Orpington and, from there, made our way to Crofton, where the Bayliss home was located. It was a pleasant enough manor - a bit on the cubic side for my personal tastes, but perfectly effective as a statement of wealth and power. Ivy softened the front, giving it a degree of charm it might otherwise have lacked, although I am quite certain it increased the costs of upkeep. Wilfred Bayliss met us himself at the door and, while he was still clearly anxious, some of the darkness under his eyes had cleared. He greeted us and offered us refreshments, which, to his obvious relief, we declined in favour of an immediate inspection.

The dining room in which the missing brother had been attacked was at the back of the house, looking out over the gardens. A row of French windows formed the entire south wall of the room, looking out onto the extensive lawns, and I could

The pleasantly ivy-laden Bayliss home

easily imagine them all opened and folded back in summer to give the pleasant illusion of dining outside. Facing them was a huge, beautifully polished mirror in a frame of twisted gold that dominated the north wall and filled the dining room with light. It was a very attractive effect. The table itself was clearly seventeenth century, with lovely lines and detailing, and the dozen accompanying chairs were either original to it or had been constructed specifically for the table by a highly talented artisan. It was as firm a statement wrought in teak as I have seen.

A slightly calmer Wilfred Bayliss

Bayliss barely seemed to see the room. He waited tensely while Holmes examined everything, including opening the doors to look out at the grounds. Eventually, he turned to Bayliss. "What, exactly, did you witness in the course of the attack?"

"Well, I was in the lounge," the fellow said. "That's this door over here." He walked over to the opposite side of the room to the one we'd entered from. "I was with Freddy. I clearly heard a gunshot - a loud one. After a moment of frozen astonishment, I leaped up, dashed across the lounge, threw open the door and charged in. Jack was approximately where you are, sir, in front of the central door, which was open. He was cowering but still on his feet. I crossed to him and he pointed out onto the grounds, trembling. He said, as I near as I can recall, 'Some bugger shot at me, Willy. I thought I was dead.' I asked him where the shot had come from and he pointed straight out across the lawn. 'He was there. Ten feet away. He stared at me for a couple of seconds, then snapped up a pistol and shot at me. I heard the bullet whistle past my bally ear. Then he took off along the side of the house.' I checked him over, made sure he was unharmed, then nervously went to look if there was any sign of the chap, but he'd escaped. Jack told me that he'd heard a noise and had opened the door to look around. He'd seen what he described as a common ruffian, a little taller and stockier than himself, dressed in cheap clothes, with unkempt hair and a scruffy beard. The police have spoken to the staff but they didn't see anyone out of place and, so far, they haven't been able to find a trace of the maniac."

"One cannot find a man who does not exist," Holmes said flatly.

Why does Holmes suggest that the attacker does not exist?

The case continues overleaf

THE BAYLISS KILLINGS

ANSWER on page 218

THE BAYLISS KILLINGS

PART THREE

Her face was the only thing visible,

pale and unhappy, but the light of zealotry

clearly burnt in her eyes.

Holmes watched as Wilfred Bayliss struggled with the revelation that his brother had faked two separate attacks on himself. Gradually, the man's face settled into grim anger. Holmes nodded. "I think it highly likely that your brother murdered your father, sir. It seems unlikely that he would kill his mother or any of his siblings, unless there is some longstanding tension that you have not mentioned, so I suspect you are safe."

"No, Mr Holmes, no particular tension. Jack is no saint, but he has no reason that I know of to wish any of us harm. Of course, I would have said the same regarding Father."

*Wilfred Bayliss, firm
and determined*

"Had anything changed in your father's life recently? Were there any disagreements between the two? Even petty ones?"

"No, not really. It was no secret that Father was disappointed about the way that Jack had been handling the firm, but that was hardly new, and it wasn't of any great significance outside the family. It doesn't make sense."

"Perhaps another member of the family might know something. They are all here today?" Holmes asked.

"More so than normal, in fact," Bayliss said. "We're all set up in the lounge. My sister Gladys took holy orders in France more than fifteen years ago. She arrived from Marseilles into Southampton port yesterday and arrived here last night. It is the first time we've seen her since her departure."

"Bereavement often brings distant family together," Holmes observed blandly. "We should speak to them, but please do avoid mention of recent revelations for a little while longer."

Bayliss's mouth thinned further but he nodded.

"Thank you," Holmes said.

Bayliss led us through to the lounge on the far side of the

dining room. It was a pleasant enough room, but my attention was captured, primarily, by the people within. Our client's mother, Florence, was huddled on the edge of an ottoman, wrapped in a thick shroud of misery and confusion. Her eyes were darting back and forth, but I doubt she saw anything of the room.

The younger brother, Frederic, was sprawled idly across a well-padded armchair, seemingly asleep. He was barely dressed, with a very loose tie and open shirt open, and his feet completely bare. He clutched a bottle of brandy in one hand and a cigarette in the other, and had clearly been indulging himself copiously in both regards. I suppose grief gave him some thin excuse for such scandalous deportment but, from the self-indulgence written across his face, it seemed quite possible this was his usual morning routine. The sister, Gladys, sat ramrod straight on a wooden chair, buried in her habit and wimple. Her face was the only thing visible, semi-veiled, pale and unhappy, but the light of zealotry clearly burnt in her eyes. It was as if all her life was concentrated in them, leeching all substance from the rest of her.

It was clear that all three children took their looks from their mother: largely anxious-looking. After a moment of awkward silence, our host nodded to himself and took a step forward. "Mother, Glad, Freddy, this is Mr Sherlock Holmes and his companion, Dr Watson. They are here to help us resolve this hideous situation. Gentlemen, please permit me to introduce my mother, Florence, my sister, Gladys and my brother, Frederic."

"Charmed," I managed. Besides me, Holmes made a polite-sounding noise.

"Our guests would like to ask a few questions," Wilfred continued.

THE BAYLISS KILLINGS

This pronouncement was met with various silences: apathetic from Frederic, intense from Gladys and confounded from Florence.

Wilfred cleared his throat awkwardly. "Yes. Well. Perhaps you would like to sit down, gentlemen?"

We did so, and a sombre-looking maid poured us some tea before retiring from the room and leaving us with just the family. Wilfred sat next to his mother on the ottoman.

Holmes took a sip of tea. "Does anyone know why any man might have borne a grudge against Augustus Bayliss?"

Frederic Bayliss as we
entered the room

Gladys, driven into
a nunnery

"Well, he was
a predatory,
overbearing prig,"
Frederic declaimed,
his voice deliberately
provocative and theatrical.

The mother didn't even look up, sunk in her despair.

Wilfred stiffened. "He gave you all the slack you could possibly want, Freddy."

"Oh, yes, he did indeed. Very generous, Daddy was. Very sanctimonious. Very disapproving. So very disappointed. But, oh, very generous."

"If you'd—" his brother began.

"If I'd what, golden boy? Followed your shining lead? Of course Father adored you. You relived his life. Strike out, work diligently, hit it big, do exactly what you were told. You never felt his spite. Not like Jack and I did. For Christ's sake, Willy, poor Gladys was driven into a silent nunnery in France, of all forsaken places." He paused for a moment. "No offence."

Gladys bobbed her head.

Frederic turned to face Holmes and me. "Our father was a shark, in a world of sharks, and prospered as sharks prosper. He was careful not to break any law of man, but I'm quite sure Gladys here could list off the laws of God and decency that he broke on a daily basis. Well, if she spoke, anyway."

"I may speak here," Gladys whispered. Her voice was thin, like paper, and scratchy with disuse. "If I must."

Frederic shrugged and took a heroic slug of brandy.

"I see," Holmes said. "And what about your missing brother, Jack?"

Frederic laughed nastily. "A chip off the paternal block, old Jacky boy. Dumb as a post, though. So, where father glided through the waters of commerce devouring all before him, Jack kept smashing his head into the hulls of ships. He didn't deserve Father's spite, but he got it anyway. It's probably for the best he died, honestly. Saved him from discovering that Father was pulling strings to get him booted from the family firm in disgrace. That damned company was Father's only true child, and Willy here was the sole fool too clueless to realize."

Holmes's face didn't so much as twitch but Wilfred went pale. I feared another eruption but Holmes stood smoothly and turned to our client. "May we have a word in the dining room, sir?"

Slightly bemused, Wilfred and I followed Holmes back into the other room. As soon as the door was closed, Bayliss started apologizing. "I'm so sorry, Mr Holmes—"

"Save your apologies, Mr Bayliss," Holmes interrupted. "They are quite inappropriate. Your brother's bitterness was most illuminating. We now know both why Jack murdered your father and where he is to be found."

What does Holmes mean?

THE BAYLISS KILLINGS

ANSWER on page 218

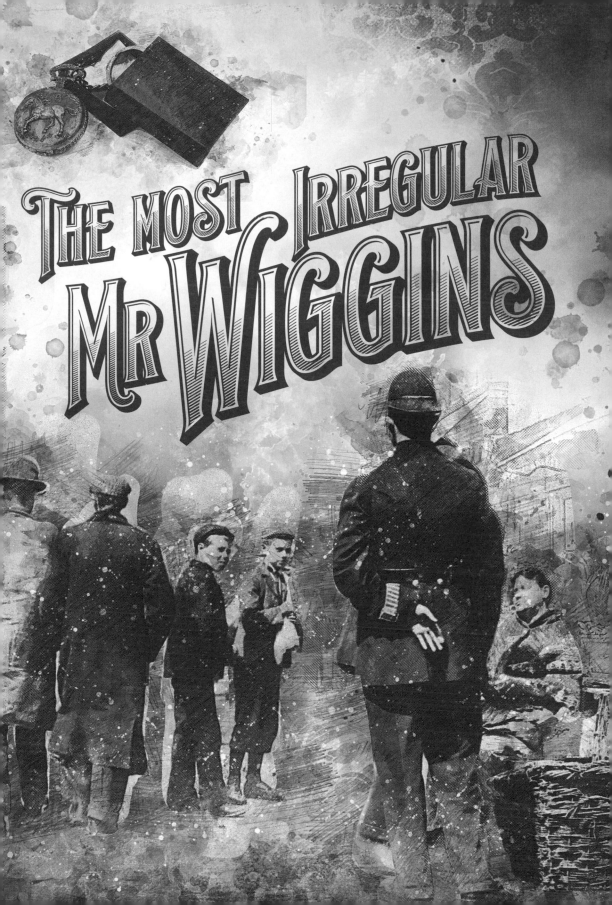

THE MOST IRREGULAR
MR WIGGINS

THE MOST IRREGULAR WIGGINS

PART ONE

"You're getting lazy, Lestrade.
I am not here to shield you from the ridiculous
expectations of your superiors."

*The return
of Lestrade*

It was late January, and winter had London in its fangs. It had been several degrees below freezing for a week straight and an icy north-easterly wind had been blowing for the last two days - one that seemed to cut straight through any amount of clothing and the flesh underneath it, to boot. So, when Lestrade arrived with another of his undistinguished cases, Holmes was not inclined to assist.

"It's an important one, Mr Holmes," the inspector protested. "Mr Chancellor is a good man, respectable and well-established, and this is a cruel blow."

"You mean he plays golf with your superintendent," Holmes snapped.

"Well, he does, yes. But that doesn't lessen his character."

Holmes raised an eyebrow. "Does it not? Is it a sign of moral fortitude now to spend one's leisure time ingratiating oneself with high-rank police officials?"

"Now, look here—" Lestrade began.

"No, inspector, I will most certainly not. This whole thing is patent nonsense. Stolen watches? Really. And despite your protestations of overwhelming complexity, it all seems plain enough that a child could solve it."

"Constable Willer is a very thorough—"

"Have you ever spoken to him? Met him, even?"

"Well, I'm sure we've—"

"Have you visited the site of the crime?"

"Not as—"

"You're getting lazy, Lestrade. I am not here to shield you from the ridiculous expectations of your superiors."

"Mr Holmes—"

"Hold." A nasty gleam appeared in Holmes's eyes and, whilst it was gone again in an instant, Lestrade looked suddenly nervous. "Very well, Lestrade. I will meet you at the warehouse in Lambeth in three hours and we will see what is required to solve this dire mystery of yours. Good day, sir."

"Right you are," Lestrade said, his voice decidedly on the uncertain side. "Three hours it is. Thank you, Mr Holmes."

As soon as the inspector had bustled down the stairs, Holmes smiled thinly. "I have a swift errand to run, Watson. I'll be back shortly." He bundled himself up and left as well.

I was none the wiser regarding Holmes's sudden and frankly lamentable about-face until we arrived at the warehouse of Chancellor's Fine Imports. Holmes got out of the carriage, and a familiarly

The familiarly ragged urchin

ragged urchin immediately detached himself from the wall and strolled over, grinning from ear to ear.

"Wiggins," Holmes said with a nod of approval. "Good of you to come."

"Wouldn't miss it for the world, Mister 'olmes," the boy said. "Afternoon, Doctor W."

"Good day, young man," I said. Wiggins was one of the most important of Holmes's network of informants; a clever and engaging scamp who ran a small gang of orphans and runaways and wielded them with the unerring instincts of a young field marshal. They were on Holmes's regular payroll and had adopted the name of The Baker Street Irregulars with a great deal of pride. A nasty thought began to blossom in my mind. "Holmes, are you—?"

"Going to let Wiggins solve this case for Inspector Lestrade in front of some of his men? Yes. I think it's high time that the inspector discovered that he needs to take a little care with his requests, lest they be fulfilled."

A couple of constables

I winced, but I did have to admit that the idea was amusing.

The three of us crossed to the gates of the warehouse grounds. Lestrade was standing there with a couple of constables and a modestly dressed fellow who I assumed to be the manager. The policemen, all three of them, gave Wiggins a very doubtful look as we approached, but none of them actually protested.

153

"Lestrade," Holmes said politely.

"Ah, Holmes," Lestrade said. "This is Mr Parker, the warehouse manager, and the constables in charge of the scene, Willer and Marshall. Gentlemen, this is Mr Sherlock Holmes, his companion Dr Watson and ... " He looked at Holmes expectantly.

"And we should examine where the thieves broke in forthwith," Holmes said, his voice impatient.

He paused a moment and I could almost see Lestrade's mental shrug. "Very well. Follow me, please. Mr Parker, could you tell Mr Holmes what you've told my lads?"

We walked briskly through an empty delivery yard and into a generous warehouse as Parker explained the situation. "Almost an entire shipment of fine Swiss watches was stolen from the warehouse last night. It's a disaster. They broke a rear window to gain access, forced open a bunch of crates, and swiped a small fortune's worth of stock. I don't know as they were looking for anything particular, given the boxes they abandoned, but they definitely liked the look of the watches."

By this point, we were approaching the back of the warehouse. The place was fairly untidy for a working environment. By the time we got to the back wall, there was a thin layer of dust visible on all the crates and surfaces. The broken window was clearly obvious, not least because of the freezing wind it allowed into the warehouse. There was little glass remaining in the frame; just a few jagged shards of no particular height.

Holmes strolled over to the window and peered at it, followed closely by Wiggins, who took pains to exaggeratedly imitate Holmes's motions and mannerisms. There was a door

Mr Parker, the warehouse manager

in the back wall some fifteen feet away, and he went over to it, still followed by Wiggins, threw back the deadbolt and went out into the small space at the back. I followed, since it was scarcely less cold outside than in. Lestrade trailed me but motioned for the manager to remain behind. One constable came with us and the other stayed inside.

An obviously broken window

The back of the warehouse was as undistinguished as the rest of the place. The wall enclosing the grounds was about seven feet high and really more of a notional barrier than an actual one to any determined crook. Other than a layer of dirt and cigarette ends, the rear space was empty.

Holmes paced around a bit, shadowed by his scruffy understudy, then turned to the lad. "Well, Wiggins?"

The penny finally dropped for Lestrade and he blanched.

"This window wasn't broken by crooks, Mr 'olmes," said Wiggins. "Not last night nor any other."

Why does Wiggins say the thieves didn't use the broken window?

The case continues opposite

THE MOST IRREGULAR Mr WIGGINS

ANSWER on page 220

THE MOST IRREGULAR WIGGINS

PART TWO

It had to be worth a princely sum - ten pounds at the very least, and possibly quite a lot more.

Lestrade looked from Wiggins to Holmes to his constable and back to Holmes, his horror bristling toward the edge of anger.

Before he could say anything, Holmes shot him the most frightfully menacing glare I've ever seen on his face. For an instant, it was as if my dear friend had been replaced by a lunatic getting ready to feast on the inspector's dripping heart. Lestrade immediately subsided, although he was clearly unhappy about the situation. I had very little sympathy for him. It really was quite cold.

"We should rejoin the dubious Mr Parker," Holmes said in his normal, crisp voice. "I trust that none of you was intending to share Wiggins's findings with him? Capital, capital." He swept back into the warehouse and up to the manager and the other policeman. "Where were the stolen goods taken from?"

Parker nodded to himself. "This way, gentlemen." He led us through a small maze of shelving and boxes, over to what would have been the left side of the warehouse if you were looking through the big front doors. "As I mentioned, they pried open a bunch of boxes before they found something they fancied the look of."

The triumphant Wiggins

Indeed, looking down the wall, I could see that there were half a dozen or more crates whose lids had been levered off and left on the floor, along with a generous portion of packing straw.

"The watches they took were over here," the manager said. He was standing next to a large open crate. A tarpaulin lining from inside the crate had been unfolded and was now spread open to dangle over the sides, and there were a number of smaller empty cardboard boxes scattered around the floor at the crate's base. The lid of the crate had been tossed to one side, and they'd obviously had some difficulty prying it up, because small splinters covered floor, boxes and tarpaulin alike.

"The crate held a dozen cardboard boxes, each of which contained six watches in shop-ready presentation cases," the manager said. "They opened a few of the boxes but, once they'd satisfied themselves that they were all the same, they just took the rest. They clearly didn't know that the shipment held eighty-four watches, though, because they didn't think to look in the small crate over there by the bench."

A handsome brown box

We obediently trailed over to have a look. "I opened this crate myself earlier to ensure the remaining watches were undisturbed." He pulled the little wooden lid off easily and unfolded the tarpaulin it contained. There were a pair of compact cardboard boxes. One had been unsealed, and he lifted the flap to show a pair of handsome brown boxes marked with a regal-looking silver crown.

"May I?" Holmes asked.

"Of course," the manager said.

Holmes reached into the cardboard box and pulled out of one of the display cases. It was

Lestrade, increasingly nervous about events

extremely elegant, slim and well constructed, the silver logo the only feature to break the dark lacquer. He examined it carefully, then opened the box to reveal a quite lovely pocket watch nestled on a bed of red velvet. It had to be worth a princely sum - ten pounds at the very least, and possibly quite a lot more. It definitely made for an impressive haul on the part of the thieves.

"Delightful," Holmes said dryly, and handed the case back to the manager.

The fellow put it back into its box carefully, folded the tarpaulin back over the boxes and put the lid back on. "You can understand why we're so distressed by this theft."

"Quite so," Holmes said. "Did the thieves, by chance, leave their pry-bar behind?"

The manager shook his head. "They used one of ours, and they took it with them, to boot. Most uncouth."

"Do you think that they knew the watches were here somewhere?"

Parker thought about that for a moment. "It's difficult to say. This shipment arrived three days ago. The thieves might have been looking for them specifically - it's no secret that Chancellor's supplies watches - but we carry a variety of goods, sometimes ones more expensive than these. It may be simply that they hoped we'd have something in here worth stealing."

"I see," Holmes said. "What about staff? How many people do you have working here?"

"There are three men who work here. I'm the manager for all of Chancellor's warehousing and supply-side business, so I run four warehouses, all reasonably close by, and attend regular meetings across London. Benjamin FitzNeal is the site supervisor. He takes care of the place while I'm elsewhere, and ensures the lads toe the line. That's Cowen and Tamson, the stockmen. They're here every day, eight through till six, with an early close on Saturdays. Chancellor's has its own delivery carts, of course, to take goods from the warehouses to the clients. They're not my direct responsibility, but we have two carts, each with a couple of lads. We didn't have any collections at this warehouse yesterday, though. No deliveries either, as I recall."

"Very good," Holmes said. "If you would be so good as to gather up to your men, we will want to interview them briefly to ascertain whether they noticed anything."

"Naturally," Parker said. "I'll return momentarily." He made his way back toward the front of the warehouse.

Holmes turned to Wiggins, ignoring Lestrade's spasm of dismay. "Your assessment, Mr Wiggins?"

"Stuff and nonsense, Mr 'olmes. That crate wasn't burgled."

Why does Wiggins say the crate wasn't burgled?

The case continues opposite

THE MOST IRREGULAR
Mr WIGGINS

ANSWER on page 220

THE MOST IRREGULAR WIGGINS

PART THREE

> "Just goes together, doesn't it, police and crime, like mash and liquor, the one following the other as natural as anything."

Holmes flashed Lestrade a quick look. The inspector had settled into a pained resignation and appeared to accept that this was an experience he was just going to have to live through.

A minute or so later, Mr Parker bustled back to where we were standing. "I've got the men standing by," he said. "Where would you like to speak to them?"

"You do not maintain an office for your own use at this location," Holmes stated.

"No," the manager said. "My office is at the Whitgift Street site."

"Then we will talk to them at the back of the warehouse. Please send your supervisor down first and keep the other two with you at the front."

"Of course."

Parker left again, with Constable Marshall in tow, and the rest of us followed Holmes down to the back wall, midway between the door and the missing window. We were out of the actual wind gusting through the hole, but it was still damnably cold. I pulled my coat a little tighter.

Poor Wiggins seemed utterly oblivious to the temperature, but I supposed he was quite accustomed to the weather. He and the other Irregulars had been working for Holmes for some time now and, as I understood the situation, maintained their ragged appearance for the sake of camouflage, rather than out of enduring necessity. The urchin must have caught my concerned examination because he winked at me and pulled up his thin, tattered coat and shirts to reveal a clean, thick woollen undergarment hidden beneath. I resolved, for the umpteenth time, to not underestimate the lad.

After a short wait, a frail old man wandered through the warehouse to approach us, mumbling to himself. He was scarcely better dressed than Wiggins, and had to be at least 75 if he was a day. There was no hint of hair beneath his cap, and I spotted a distinct hint of palsy about his hands.

The manager continued to appear helpful

Constable Willer nodded at him and said, "Inspector, gentlemen, this is Mr FitzNeal, the supervisor."

"That I am, sirs, that I am. Benjamin FitzNeal at your service, but you should feel free to call me Ben or Fitz or really anything else, so long as it's not too shockingly rude, and I'm sure it wouldn't be, not with all you fine young men being so clearly upstanding." He blinked at Wiggins. "And, my word, you bobbies do start young, don't you? No disrespect intended, constable - or, I don't know, maybe you're a sergeant - everyone looks young to my old eyes, and very pleased I am to be living in a world where fine young fellows like yourself can get paid to look after the interests of us common folk too, I must say, but—"

"Mr FitzNeal," Holmes said sharply.

"That's my name, and I'll thank you—"

"Sir!" Holmes snapped.

The old man blinked and fell silent for a moment.

Before he could start talking again, Holmes leapt in: "What happened here last night?"

"Oh, of course, you would want to know about that, good sir, wouldn't you, what with you being the police and all, and a crime having been committed. Just goes together, doesn't it, police and crime, like mash and liquor, the one following the other as natural as anything. Terrible business, crime is. Terrible. I'm not quite sure what the world is coming to, to tell you the truth. Why, just last week, my—"

"Last night, sir," Holmes said loudly and firmly.

I glanced over at Wiggins and saw that he was watching the supervisor with a fascinated intensity.

"Last night!" exclaimed FitzNeal, standing a little straighter, or at least hunching slightly less. "Ruffians broke in through that there very window, so they did. Smashed it into little smithereens.

BANG!" His sudden bellow startled us all. "CRASH! WALLOP! Let themselves into our poor warehouse all sneaky and horrible, and made off with, um, watches! Terrible business, and I give thanks to the great Lord above that none of us were here at the time, oh no, all safely away and tucked in bed, we were, miles away, and, if we hadn't been, then who can guess as to what horrible fate might have befallen us. Wallop! Not good at all, no, not good at all. Why, my lad Tom's oldest got into a terrible ruckus when he was little more than a stripling himself, and he never did get the hearing back in that ear afterward. Some hooligan jammed a sharp stone in there good and proper, and they got that out all right, otherwise he'd look a bit strange now, wouldn't he, wandering around with a rock sticking out of his—"

"Thank you, sir," Holmes said clearly. "Please tell Mr Cowen to join us."

"Right you are," FitzNeal said and immediately began shuffling away, still talking. I heard, "Mr Cowen to go down to the nice gentlemen next, right as rain, I'm sure he'll ... " before the sound of the old man's voice faded into obscurity.

Holmes pinched the bridge of his nose.

We stood there in silence for a period of time, somewhat dazed. Well, I felt dazed, at least, and Lestrade looked rather like he'd wish the ground would just swallow him up.

Some moments later, Cowen appeared. He was a burly lad of about twenty, with short hair and a bushy beard. The constable introduced him and he nodded to us in greeting.

The newly-promoted constable

"Could you tell us what happened here last night?" Holmes asked after a moment.

"A robbery, sirs." His voice was low and reluctant and, for a moment, I feared that was going to be the extent of what he said, but he continued on. "Broke that window. Sneaked on inside. Looked around some. Popped some boxes. Stole the watches. We was home. Fitz arrived first. He called help." He paused momentarily again. "Sirs?"

Holmes sighed. "Yes, yes, you can go. I'll send someone to ask your colleague, Mr Tamson, to join us."

"Thank you, sir," Cowen managed. He nodded respectfully again and padded off.

"I shudder to imagine what we might expect from the third fellow," Holmes said. "A compulsive stutter, perhaps? An urge to declaim every statement in iambic pentameter, whether or not the metre fits the words?" He turned to Wiggins. "Do we need to speak to our remaining unfortunate?"

Wiggins shook his head. "Not in the least, Mr 'olmes. They're all lying through their teeth. My money's on that manager, but I'm sure the inspector 'ere will find the ringleader in no time."

Why does Wiggins say that they are all lying?

THE MOST IRREGULAR Mr WIGGINS

ANSWER on page 220

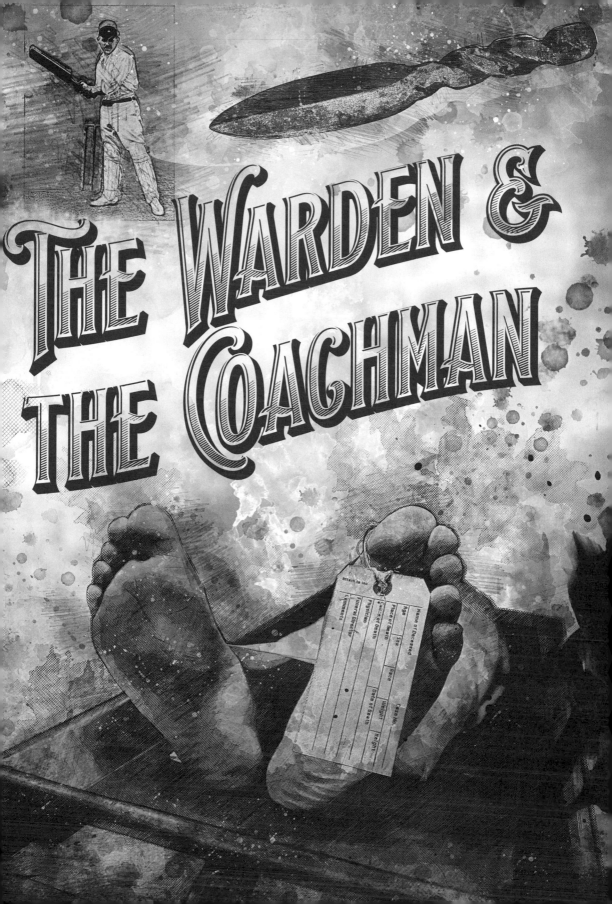

THE WARDEN AND THE COACHMAN

PART ONE

"His idea of a perfect evening was a hot pot of tea,
a roaring fire and a brand-new book."

Warden & Riley was a successful firm of carriage manufacturers who supplied vehicles to London clients, big and small alike. They had a range of options that included heavy-duty working coaches through to bespoke luxury conveyances for the discerning gentleman about town. I'd never heard of them, having not the least interest in who manufactured the cabs I rode in, but Holmes claimed to at least be aware of them - something to do with heights and types of paint, but I confess I wasn't entirely listening when he explained.

The reason I had become aware of them at all was that James Warden, one of the founders of the firm, was in the process of explaining his frustrations regarding the police investigation into the murder of Kenneth Riley, the other founder of the firm. Warden was in his fifties, a man clearly used to taking command

of situations and having his directions followed. To see him at such a helpless loss now was oddly moving.

"Kenneth was found murdered in a filthy alley off Bethnal Green Road," Warden told us. "According to the Whitechapel police, it's a particularly wretched stretch known almost exclusively for opium, whoring and bare-knuckle fighting dens. Lots of bodies turn up in the area. He was stabbed, and they assume it's just bad luck. He was a gentle, quiet man. Shy, even. His idea of a perfect evening was a hot pot of tea, a roaring fire and a brand-new book. I knew him better than his own brother did. If he was mixed up in something, he would have sought my help. He had done so before and knew I would never judge him unkindly. It makes absolutely no sense for him to have been in such a squalid place."

Holmes nodded thoughtfully. "It might be useful, in this instance, to see if we can learn anything from the body. We should go to Whitechapel."

"I will accompany you, if I may," Warden said. "If you have any questions, it will be easier for you to ask them if I am there in person."

"Very well," Holmes said, somewhat to my surprise.

Less than half an hour later, we pulled up outside the police station on Commercial Street. It was a long, thin, three-storey building with stone cladding on the ground floor that ran along the pavement for the best part of a hundred feet. The scene outside was chaotic, with people of all sorts milling around, most of them unhappy, and a constant stream of policemen coming and going. From what I could tell, a good proportion of the people in the vicinity were drunk, drugged, or both. The noise was as ferocious as the stench.

Holmes pushed through the hubbub, and Warden and I followed in his wake. Inside, the station was scarcely more orderly. Holmes elbowed through to the front desk and had a brief shouted conversation with a fellow on the other side. The chap waved us off to the right and, after a few moments, we found ourselves in a small, untidy room with a couple of writing tables and a smattering of chairs. An uncomfortable twenty minutes later, an older constable brought in a cardboard box and put it on a table.

"Effects in the Riley murder for Mr Holmes," the fellow said in a broad Devon accent. "Constable Fennel had to rush himself off to a robbery but he said as you're welcome to look it all over, so long as you don't take nowt. He said he'd be glad for a note if you spot anything. I'll take it back after, but I don't know first thing about any of it, sorry to say, so if you've got questions, you'll need to wait for him."

Holmes thanked the man and we went to take a look. The box contained the dead man's clothes

*Some of the dead
man's effects*

- a rather nice felt hat in dark
grey, a pair of fashionably narrow
and well-polished black leather shoes
with an inch of heel, a heavy wool lounge suit
the same colour as the hat, a pair of black leather
gloves, a white cotton shirt, and a black knee-length
wool topcoat with a dark-grey fur trim. It was an elegant
ensemble, even marred as it was by the gash in the clothing
and the mud covering the front of the coat and trousers. The
only other items in the box were a money clip containing a
moderate sum, and a crude dagger.

Holmes picked the dagger up and examined it curiously.
It really was a shoddy piece of work, with an unusually wide
and simple blade, a simple handle moulded out of iron, and
absolutely no cross guard whatsoever. I'd never seen anything

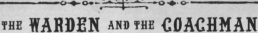
like it - it must have been sold very cheaply indeed. There was a certain horrific brutality to it, though. A weapon for murder, for sure, rather than for fighting or cooking - or anything else - really.

Flourishing it at the startled constable, Holmes said, "Seen anything like this before?"

"No, sir," the man said. "Not a once." He rallied a little and took a second look. "Ugly piece of crap, um, if you'll pardon my French."

"Exactly so, constable." Holmes set the knife down thoughtfully. "Well, we know for sure he wasn't killed in that alley."

How can Holmes be so certain that Riley was murdered elsewhere?

The case continues overleaf

THE WARDEN & THE COACHMAN

ANSWER on page 221

THE WARDEN AND THE COACHMAN

PART TWO

"Are you suggesting he was murdered because of a cricket match?"

Holmes turned to the constable who was with us. "Is Mr Riley's body in the building still, Constable ... ?"

"Nolan, sir. I expect so, given that the effects are here, but I can't promise you it's the case."

"Would you be so kind as to show us to the coroner's offices, Constable Nolan? I will write a report out for your Constable Fennel afterward, detailing our findings."

Nolan shrugged. "Can't see as there's any harm in it, sir. This way, if you would."

The constable picked up the box of effects, took us through the building and down into an extensive basement area. The morgue was tucked away through a pair of double doors. It was spacious, well lit and chilly, all of which I had expected, and also tidy and organized, which was a pleasant surprise. The coroner came over, introduced himself as Eric Ryan, and immediately agreed to let Holmes and me have a look at the body.

"I'm sure you know how it is, doctor," he said to me. "We're all drowning in work here. Right across Division H, in fact. It's not quite so bad down here in the morgue, but the police officers are all constantly running after their own tails just trying to keep up. So I'm happy to take any extra consultation that's available."

Warden excused himself to wait outside while Dr Ryan fetched the body. Riley had been five foot ten and slimly built. The cause of death was obvious - a wide, ugly stab wound to the central trunk, with some curious black discolouration on the skin toward the centre of the wound. A knife was clearly responsible for the stab wound, and it had gone clean through the aortic iliac junction, causing massive blood loss. The best that could be said of it was that shock would have been instant and death would have followed very swiftly.

Constable Nolan

"I don't see any disease indicators," I remarked.

"No," Dr Ryan said. "The victim was in good condition. He could have done with a little more exercise, perhaps, but, for his age, he was doing well."

"He was a keen cricketer," Holmes observed. "Look at the index fingers of both hands. Those calluses are a sure sign of a deep batsman and come from the repeated impact of ball against bat. Not much evidence of fielding impact, so he wasn't much use in the slip. Probably left somewhere deep when his side were fielding. All amateur, of course, or else he'd be fitter, but I imagine he had some raw talent."

The body of Kenneth Riley

"Fascinating," said Dr Ryan. "Anything else?"

"Well, you can see how fastidious he was. Look at the trimming at the cuticles and the plucked pores around the eyebrows. This was a man who took care to present himself to the world precisely as he intended to. There's some evidence of an old knee injury visible on the sole of the foot, but it clearly wasn't enough to stop him playing cricket, or else the calluses would have faded. Perhaps he was allowed a runner."

Riley was a keen cricketer

"Are you suggesting he was murdered because of a cricket match?" I asked.

"Try to pay attention, Watson. Of course not. It's not impossible, but I don't see any reason to suspect that here."

"Right," I said.

"Thank you for your time, Dr Ryan," Holmes said.

"My pleasure, sir," Ryan replied. "It was most educational."

We rejoined Warden outside the morgue. "Did you learn anything?" he asked.

"We learned that Kenneth was a keen cricketer," I said.

"Oh, yes, that he was. Played every Sunday without fail. He used to be quite something, but he damaged his leg in a nasty fall and that hampered him. Didn't stop him enjoying the sport. He didn't really socialize with the team or other players outside of games, though. Like I said, he was somewhat shy. Well, awkward more than shy, I suppose. His teammates didn't seem to mind."

"I assume you'd have mentioned any enemies or rivals or other potential sources of suspicion by now," I said.

"Of course," Warden said. "Kenneth really wasn't the sort of man to develop enemies. There were some fools who were jealous of his talent twenty years ago, and our company definitely has rivals, just as any business does, but he'd been a manager for twelve years. Killing him doesn't hurt the firm. Just me."

"What do you know of the brother?" Holmes asked.

"Carl. He lives up in Manchester, as does their mother, Emily. He's a painter and decorator. Their father was a builder. He died five or six years ago now. Kenneth wasn't particularly close to them, but they had a fond relationship and he spent Christmas with them most years."

Holmes nodded to himself. "No wife, of course."

"No," agreed Warden. "Kenneth was fond of his quiet time and perfectly self-sufficient."

"I would think so," Holmes said. "Our most pressing concern at this point is to uncover the murder weapon."

What does Holmes mean?

THE WARDEN &
THE COACHMAN

The case continues opposite

ANSWER on page 221

THE WARDEN AND THE COACHMAN

PART THREE

All manner of banging, clangs,
roaring flames, and so on.

arden looked at Holmes in evident confusion. "Who the devil uses a red-hot weapon?"

"With a few odd exceptions, someone who is not planning violence and who has a piece of red-hot metal close to hand."

"Yes, I suppose so," Warden said.

"I assume you must work with at least a few forges and foundries professionally?"

"Of course," Warden said.

"Any in the East End?"

The man thought for a moment. "Roger Edmunds has a foundry on Whitechapel High Street. He specializes in decorative iron and steel. I don't know why Kenneth would have been there on Tuesday, though."

"Let us enquire forthwith," Holmes said.

The metalworks was just a hundred yards down Whitechapel High Street from the Royal London Hospital, a pleasantly prosperous area by the standards of East London - not Bond Street by any means, of course, but not Bethnal Green either. The streets were busy, but without any of the chaos we'd seen outside the Commercial Street station.

Mr Edmunds met us in a small office at the back of his metalworks. It was, unsurprisingly,

Metalworker Roger Edmunds
in his foundry

a very noisy establishment – all manner of banging, clangs, roaring flames, and so on – but his office was, fortunately, well insulated from the clatter, so we were able to hear ourselves think. Edmunds himself was a tidy man in his thirties, with short hair and a well-trimmed beard. He was of moderate height but extremely muscular in the arms, shoulders and chest.

"Tuesday? No, I haven't seen Mr Riley since I delivered that scrollwork railing to you last month," he told Warden. "I left a little early on Tuesday evening, though. If he came by after five p.m., I'd have missed him."

"How many men were still here when you left on Tuesday?" Holmes asked.

"Dandison and Hanna would have been here until seven p.m., sir," Edmunds said. "Later if they were in the middle of a piece, possibly. Bennett's on six to four this week, and Marcus took a half-day because his mum was poorly. Would you like me to ask them?"

"Would you mind if I spoke to them personally?" said Holmes.

Edmunds glanced at Warden's concerned expression. "Of course not."

"Capital," Holmes said. "If you'd be so good as to point us toward Mr Dandison then?"

The fellow took us through the metalworks to a large, hot, smoky forge area. It was one of several stations within the sprawling,

Metal fresh from the forge

high-roofed building, and comprised two different furnaces with automatic bellows, anvils in three sizes, two very heavy wooden benches replete with an assortment of clamps and tools, and a multiplicity of barrels containing water, oil and possibly other substances. It was an impressive set-up. Several pieces of metal were on the coals.

Dandison turned out to be a younger, better-looking version of his boss - early twenties, with a square jaw, green eyes and high cheekbones, and every bit as massively strong. He was wearing a short-sleeved shirt under a heavy leather apron and leather gauntlets that reached up to his mid forearm. Even so, the rest of his visible arms were covered in old burns.

"You know, I think, maybe I did see Mr Riley late on Tuesday," Dandison said. "He didn't come in, though. He was by the gate, talking to another fellow. I didn't think anything of it. No, I couldn't hear them over the din in here, and I only ever saw the other man's back. There was some gesticulating, though, and then they got into a coach together. This must have been half past seven, I suppose. I was finishing up some railings. What did he look like? The other fellow, you mean? Like I said, I didn't get a look at his face, but he was dressed very nicely, expensive suit, silk shirt, a thick, dark wool greatcoat and a tall topper. A gentleman, or someone determined to look the part. He was probably a little under six feet, from the brim of his hat. Medium build, I suppose. Actually, I can tell you that the coach they got into was from Grahams'. We make their running gear."

Holmes thanked the man and had him direct us to Mr Hanna, the other man on duty. Like the other two, he was immensely muscular. He was older, though, past fifty, his face cracked and seamed. His work area was similar to Dandison's, varying chiefly in the placements of its components. He also had a third table laden with much smaller tools and anvils, suggesting some surprisingly fine work.

"Yes, I was here," he said grudgingly. "No, I didn't see Mr Riley or anyone else, on account of I spends my time working, rather than staring out the bleeding door. I left at seven sharp. Yes, Dandison was still here, buggering about with some work he shouldn't have started as late as he did. He'll learn. Presumably. What? Yes, of course I'd know a Grahams' coach if I saw one. I didn't see one and, no, I didn't see no gentleman neither. There could have been a parade of them go past outside, in fact. Like I said, I was working. Which is what I need to be doing right now, if you'll permit me."

Holmes murmured his thanks and we withdrew.

"Frank Hanna has always been far lovelier in metal than he is in conversation," Warden said apologetically.

"He was very useful," Holmes said. "We may not understand the reasons yet, but the killer's identity is quite plain."

Who does Holmes think the murderer is?

THE WARDEN & THE COACHMAN

ANSWER on page 221

THE CASE OF THE INDIAN TIGER

PART ONE

"When we discovered this morning that
he had been violently murdered, my mother
broke down sobbing. In joy."

Miss Eunice Albinson was a fine-featured young woman of slight stature and, whilst her clothes were of the highest quality and cut in the latest fashions, there was a sense of ephemerality that clung to her. She was clearly distressed, but she appeared more concerned than grief-stricken and, as her conversation with Holmes progressed, she was getting steadily more worried.

"My father's will is very specific," she said. "Even though he was retired, in the event of his death at home or at any other location within London, any bequest is utterly dependent on your investigation of the circumstances. A generous sum is allotted for your time."

"I recognize those facts, Miss Albinson," Holmes replied. "The fact remains, however, that I have never heard of Jeremiah Turner Albinson, he certainly had no arrangement with me, and the specifics of his will do not inspire the slightest interest in me."

She sagged, clearly wishing that the earth would open to swallow her up, but she persisted. "Perhaps you don't understand," she began, and Holmes stiffened in quiet outrage. "Ah," she managed. "That is, maybe I have been insufficiently clear. If you don't help us, all of Father's money and possessions pass in perpetuity to the trust of his bank. My mother, my siblings and I would all be completely destitute."

"My dear lady, I sympathize, but I am hardly responsible—"

"My father was a monster," she blurted. "There. I said it. When we discovered this morning that he had been violently murdered, my mother broke down sobbing. In joy. Then, of course, his lawyer arrived and explained that, unless you specifically scrutinized his death and pronounced us innocent of it, we would be out on the streets by nightfall. It is utterly characteristic of his mind. I never heard of anyone having a good word to say about him in all of his sixty-five years. He was an appalling human being in every respect, and even his cronies cordially loathed him, as they loathe every other person who is not themselves. If my siblings and I are still able to walk and talk and venture forth in public like normal human beings, it is only because he spent too much time in India to have the opportunity to shatter us more completely. This is his last revenge on us, and a grossly humiliating accusation that one of us is a murderer. I assure you that we are nothing of the sort. We are not like him. Please do not give the vile old beast his last victory. Please. Help us."

"I intensely dislike being strong-armed," Holmes said, "but it seems that you are not the one at fault in that regard. Very well."

An hour later, we were at the Albinson home on Sheldrake Place, looking west over Holland Park, which stretched out, green and lovely, for almost a third of a mile. It was a delightful property, originally part of the Phillimore estate. The building was reasonably compact, but the elegance of its design and the prestige of its history were more than lavish, and town houses do, of necessity, tend to be less sprawling than estates in the home counties. The interior decoration proved somewhat vulgar, which I had rather expected. It was, at least, softened here and there by attempts at taste and understatement. It gave the place a somewhat fractured feel.

Miss Albinson gave us into the care of the butler, Carey, almost as soon as we arrived. She explained that she did not usually reside at the house and had not been there the day before so was not best placed to provide information. She

Miss Eunice Albinson

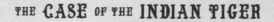

entreated him to be absolutely open and honest with us in all particulars and went to care for her mother.

Holmes asked to be shown the location of the murder before anything else, and Carey took us to a large, tasteless study on the first floor with an attractive view over the park. It was clear that a titanic struggle had taken place in the room, and drying blood was everywhere. The smell was quite ghastly. There wasn't a single piece of furniture left untouched, and books and papers had been strewn all over the room. The desk had been pushed to a peculiar angle, the leather writing surface stained with wine and blood. Its accompanying balloon-back chair had been thrown over and, when Holmes righted it, I saw that it had a gash right through the back and that one of its arms had been removed. A bookcase had been completely upturned, several paintings had been smashed, one armchair had been partially launched into the fire - which must, fortunately, have been unlit - and the other had been hacked at wildly. The standing lamp had actually been snapped in two. Holmes paced around the chaos, a calculating expression on his face.

After a time, he rejoined Carey and me by the door. "You saw the body?" he asked.

"Yes, sir," the butler said.

"It is clear to me that you are a former military man - a sergeant, I fancy. You were also once a skilled

Carey, the butler

Snapped in two

and enthusiastic amateur boxer, though I see that you have not fought in the ring with any regularity for twelve years or so. Would you consider yourself familiar with wounds and corpses?"

He hesitated a moment, clearly startled. "Yes, sir, I suppose I am."

"In your formerly professional capacity, then, what do you think Dr Watson and I would note if were we to inspect the body?"

Carey thought about it. "He'd been smashed around a lot, sir, but it was the stabbing that killed him. The bludgeoning came after. He was cut on the arms plenty and stabbed a dozen times or more - six in the chest, four in the stomach, one in the back, two in the groin - and had several deep cuts to the face. There was a lot of blood, as you can see. It must have been one hell of a fight."

"Oh, I think we can rule a fight out," Holmes said.

Why does Holmes doubt that there was a fight?

The case continues overleaf

THE CASE OF THE INDIAN TIGER

ANSWER on page 222

THE CASE OF THE INDIAN TIGER

PART TWO

"My only surprise is that it has taken six years for vengeance to follow him back to London."

Carey looked troubled. "I find it disturbing that someone was able to fake such a mess in here."

"Is it any less disturbing than the idea that a mighty brawl took place in here without your knowledge?" Holmes asked.

"No, I suppose not. But it is, somehow, more invasive ... more unsettling."

"I dare say. Your former employer was, according to Miss Albinson, not a man of fine character."

The butler snorted. "You could say that."

"So there would be plenty of people who would have reason to murder him?"

"Anyone who'd ever met the old beast," Carey said.

"Yet you were in his service."

"Six years, for my sins." The man shook his head wearily.

The troubled Carey

"I was, as you surmised, a sergeant in Her Majesty's army. Ten years, including Afghanistan and India, and, while I did not cross Albinson's path there, I did hear of his ... work. There is a certain kind of man who takes to active service as a way of filling a dark need he cannot otherwise fill legally. You find them in rank and file, black-souled devils whose only emotion is a bleak joy in the agony of others. One gets used to dealing with them, in a way. Thanks to my experience, I was able to survive Albinson, slightly deflect some of his excesses toward the maids and, in the process, spare some other, less able wretch from having to serve in my stead." He bowed his head a little. "Perhaps I also thought that the unpleasantness of my position may offer me some atonement for regrettable past duties."

"What did Albinson do in India?" Holmes asked.

"He ravaged Assam, sir. There is no other word for it. When a tea baron wished to expand his plantation, Albinson was one of those monsters who ensured that the territory they sought was unoccupied. The poor devils he and his men fell upon would have been well served by taking their own lives at the mere sight of him. It would have spared them much agony and torment. My only surprise is that it has taken six years for vengeance to follow him back to London."

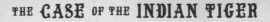

"You think the killer is from India, despite the apparent plenitude of ill-wishers?"

"I know it, sir. In Assam, Albinson eventually fell foul of a bandit who called himself the Tiger - a tall, powerful man with a mane of black hair whose family had been slain by Albinson's men. For the five years leading up to Albinson's retirement, the Tiger hunted him tirelessly. Despite every precaution, the bandit killed dozens of the old man's guards and cut-throats, burnt a palace down around his ears and came within a whisker of skewering him twice. Late yesterday afternoon, I glanced out across the park and saw a tall, muscular Indian man highlighted by the setting sun. He had long, shaggy black hair and was standing in the park, just staring at the house. He looked to be dressed in a suit. I did not say anything to my employer - he was already paranoid and rage-prone, and a warning would only have inflamed him. Instead, I claimed a headache, went to bed and took a stiff dose of laudanum to ensure I would pass out and not be easily disturbed." He must have noted my disapproval because he added, "It is a medication I keep strictly for emergencies, doctor."

"And you are sure that this nemesis is the source of his undoing?" Holmes asked.

"Quite certain," Carey said. "The man kept telling stories about the Tiger, the way one prods at a painful tooth. I've heard a steady stream

The Tiger

of them. I think he considered the man's attentions, much as he disliked them, as a medal celebrating his achievements."

"Hmm. And where were you employed before Albinson?"

"I worked for Lord Tomkins in Hampshire. He was a delightful old boy, considerate and generous. I was in his service for most of a decade. He died about the same time that Albinson returned from India. The previous butler here held out for three days after his master's return. I fell into the role, learnt what it was and made my uneasy peace with it. By the end of my first fortnight, Mrs Albinson had managed to secure permission for the children to spend most of the week with her sister's family in Kent. They were forced to slink back for weekends, like whipped curs, but they got to escape again on Sunday evening. If only the rest of the household could have had similar escape."

"You have suggested that your employer was abusive to the maids."

"He was abusive to everyone, but he was grotesquely vile to the unfortunate women who tried to work here. I warned every woman I interviewed, and I got in the way of his attentions as much as possible, but there was only so much that I could do.

The sensible ones lasted less than a week, fleeing as soon as they took his full measure. There were always more who were so needy that they'd take the job, though. The more easily broken or more desperate lasted a few weeks here - maybe a month or two. One particularly tragic young woman managed to endure for almost six months, but there was some deep urge for self-destruction in her. Cooks were harder to recruit - within a year, no one would touch the position with a barge pole - and Mrs Albinson was bullied into cooking. It is not a skill she possesses, even now, five years later."

"And the current maid?"

He sighed. "Annet Webster. She's been here three weeks. She would have broken already if not for her mother's ill health. I was very concerned about her."

Holmes pinched the bridge of his nose. "I feel for your plight, man, but lying to me will not help your case one whit. The truth will out and, if you continue to attempt to obscure it, my sympathies will, very swiftly, evaporate."

Why does Holmes think the butler is lying?

The case continues overleaf

THE CASE OF THE INDIAN TIGER

ANSWER on page 222

THE CASE OF THE INDIAN TIGER

PART THREE

"His misdeeds finally caught up to him, as they were, most certainly, going to do sooner or later."

The butler stiffened for a moment and then sagged slightly. "Very well, sir. I did not definitively see the Tiger in the park. But I felt his eyes on me, and what I could see was certainly a plausible fit for the man. If I have taken a degree of poetic license in that regard, it is nothing more than my absolute certainty regarding Mr Albinson's killer." He straightened again, and the light of conviction burnt strongly in his eyes. "His misdeeds finally caught up to him, as they were, most certainly, going to do sooner or later."

Holmes scrutinized the fellow for several seconds. "I see," he said, but precisely what it was that my old friend saw remained uncertain. "I will need to talk to everyone else who was in the house last night, of course."

Stiffened for

a moment

"Of course," Carey said, a professional neutrality slipping over his face like a mask. "That will be Annet and Mrs Albinson."

"Excellent," Holmes said. "If you could fetch the girl?"

"I hardly think this is a seemly location for an interview with a badly shaken young woman, sir. She has suffered far too much already."

Holmes arched an eyebrow. "Where would you suggest?"

"The parlour," the butler said flatly.

"Very well," Holmes said.

Carey took us to the parlour, his face still stiff and formal, and left us there while he went to get the maid. Like the rest of the house, the parlour was a curious mix of gaudy and restrained, typified in a horrendously out-of-place turquoise-veneered low table with gold inlay, which had been covered with a lace tablecloth, a runner and various books. I was still eyeing that thing when the butler ushered the maid in.

"Thank you for speaking with us," Holmes told her. He gave the butler a stern glance. "That will be all for now, Carey."

The man was clearly unhappy, but he left the room and closed the door behind him. The maid sagged a little at his departure. She was a slip of a thing, poorly fed, with very pale skin and a shock of red hair attempting to escape her bonnet. It was clear that she'd been handled roughly. There were bruises of varying ages visible on her face and neck, including a recent one to her left cheek. Her hands had also suffered, with one finger that looked as if it had been wrenched recently, a livid red bruise along the top of her right thumb and the edge of her hand either side of the knuckle, and an ageing but nasty bruise on her left wrist, as if fingers had dug between the bones of her forearm. The tentative movement of each step she took spoke volumes about the pain she was in elsewhere in her body.

"Please sit down, Miss Webster," Holmes said, his voice carefully neutral.

The maid
Annet Webster

She shuddered, but obeyed.

"What happened last night?" Holmes asked.

The girl flinched. "There was a terrible ruckus, sir. Late, it was. I'm not sure when. I ... I hid. In my room. I couldn't say how long it went on for. Then, this morning ... I thought it was some sort of cruel game at first." For an instant, a passion shook her body. "I'm glad he's dead."

"That seems a common sentiment," Holmes observed.

Annet flinched again but said nothing.

"You've been here three weeks?" he asked.

"Yes, sir."

"And, apart from hiding in your room, what else happened last night?"

"I don't know, sir. I was attending Mrs Albinson all evening. She felt ill after dinner and asked that I sit with her in her rooms. Eventually, she decided to go to sleep, and I went to my bed myself."

"Thank you," Holmes said. "That will be all for now. If you would ask Mrs Albinson to join us?"

The maid stood and bobbed a curtsy. "Yes, sir."

A minute or two later, the mistress of the house came in. We stood and exchanged introductions. Mrs Albinson was in her late forties and had clearly been a handsome woman once. Traces of her former beauty were still visible beneath the hollow-eyed affliction. She bore fewer bruises than the maid had, but there were scars visible on eyebrow, cheek and hand, and one of her index fingers had clearly been broken and reset at a very odd angle. It looked like a significantly uncomfortable impediment to daily life.

"I thank you for coming at my late husband's presumptuous instructions," she said to us. "I am as grateful for your presence as I am resentful that it has been imposed on me."

Holmes nodded. "I would imagine nothing less, madam. Can you tell me what happened last night?"

"The grotesque villain met a richly deserved end," she said frankly. "And whatever happens to me next, it will be better than sharing his roof. Even if that means starving in the gutter."

"Yes, quite. I was rather hoping for your specific recollections, however."

"At dinner, I told my husband that I felt ill and needed Annet to attend me. Then she and I went to my room, where she sat with me

Mrs Albinson

and did some needlepoint whilst I read. I did offer her a book, but she's not much of a reader, the poor dear. My frequent headaches were, as I'm sure you can guess, a flimsy excuse to get the girl away from that beast, and had been going on ever since his return. He was always an animal but that last stint in India had eroded the final shreds of restraint he'd once possessed. Eventually, I went to sleep. I heard some disturbance at one point, prayed to God that it was my husband being slain, and went back to sleep. Incredibly, it seems my prayer was answered."

"Yes, well, I think I've learnt all I need to," Holmes said. "The identity of the killer is perfectly clear. I assume the lawyers your daughter spoke of will wish to speak to me?"

Mrs Albinson did her best to hide it, but I clearly saw the spasm of fear that shot through her before she got it under control. "Yes. I will send for Mr Howe. May I be permitted to ask what you will tell them?"

Holmes sighed. "I cannot, in conscience, do other than tell them that your husband was assassinated by the Tiger, an Indian enemy come to bring vengeance upon him for the horrors of his past. But I pray, do not insult me further by pretending that you or I believe it."

Who does Holmes believe to be the actual killer?

THE CASE OF THE INDIAN TIGER

ANSWER on page 222

THE MYSTERY OF SIR WILLOUGHBY

PART ONE

If he shot himself fatally through the heart, how did he place the gun cleanly on top of the suicide note in a desk tidy afterward? The scene must have been staged.

PART TWO

"Your people have done a fine job of cleaning the room, Sir Willoughby, but they neglected to empty the fireplace - perfectly understandable, given their distress and the fact that the study would be unlikely to see use in the immediate future." Holmes produced a brass shell with a flourish. "This held the bullet whose report you heard. It was placed in the grate, embedded inside something - most likely a piece of wood - to prevent its immediate explosion. You can see the hole it made in the wall over there. The bullet itself is still embedded in the brick because the hole is dark. Your father was killed silently, almost certainly with a weapon designed to leave a hole that could be mistaken for a bullet wound - an ice-pick chosen to match the correct diameter, for example. It would be trivial to put a previously discharged bullet into the wound afterward."

PART THREE

I was still trying to form a sensible answer for Holmes when Sir Willoughby returned.

"I'm afraid that Alexander murdered your father," Holmes told the man.

"But ... " spluttered Willoughby, aghast.

"He knew your father was working on papers. You didn't tell him about them, I assume?"

"No ... " His face hardened, and I wondered that I had ever thought the man looked like a grocer. Now he was every inch the son of a judge: stern, and as unyielding as granite.

"They were under the body, obliterated by the blood, then thrown away once the corpse was removed. You've said only yourself, Baker and Rowlands were involved in the tidying. Lawrence and Ronald did not recall their presence enough to mention them and were unsure what your father had been doing that day. The only way your brother can know of the papers is if he is the murderer. If you look into Alexander's finances, I think you will find significant irregularities. You should also talk to his solicitor and ask whether he mentioned changing his will."

Following Holmes's advice, Willoughby dealt with the matter carefully, assembling evidence before confronting his brother. Alexander had fallen into the clutches of an unshakeable gambling habit. His father had financed his desperation for a time then, regretfully, decided to cut him out of the family finances - the document he was working on when he was killed, most likely. When faced with the evidence, Alexander swiftly confessed.

THE FLAME OF BANGKOK

PART ONE

The iron bars have a maximum gap of two-and-a-half inches, and they are still in place. The thief must have reached through the bars, which would require a slender arm. The suspects all have physically demanding jobs and are likely to be too muscular to get their arms through.

PART TWO

"Clearly, it is impossible for someone to have dashed through a dark shop and across the rear room to the vault, and then unlock it and open it enough to squeeze an arm through the security bars, retrieve a specific item and then hide, all in the space of twenty seconds. If we eliminate the impossible, as we must, then the answer is clear: the thief was already in place. Do you open and scrutinize the cleaning closet in your back room as part of your routine, sir?"

Cutler's eyes were round with astonishment. "Well, I'll be damned."

"It seems unlikely that even the sternest vicar would consider a minor error in procedure to be a mortal sin. The thief was in the closet before you closed for the night. As soon as you went upstairs, he or she set to work opening the vault door, then greased the arm used to snatch the stone, and retrieved it. The alarm sounded when he or she opened the door to depart the shop."

PART THREE

"My dear fellow, you did notice that all of the valuables in Cutler's vault are in one of two types of identical package, did you not?"

I nodded.

"The thief must have known precisely which one to take. The absence of discarded pouches and cases proves it. He bought himself time by hiding in the closet, but not an infinite amount, so some circumspection was required. Only one person other than Cutler was working on site both before and after the stone arrived. It doesn't matter whether he carefully watched where Cutler put it, or whether he made sure to study the contents of the vault before and then looked for a new item afterward. Either way, Edmund Gregson is the only one who could possibly have known which item to steal. I have no doubt his friends will alibi him strongly, but also no doubt that they will recant when Lestrade explains the grave seriousness of this investigation."

It was as Holmes said. Gregson's friends insisted he was with them in the pub until Lestrade started talking about treason. Then they all quickly said that he'd paid them well for the alibi. Shortly after that, Gregson confessed to having been paid a shockingly large sum of money to steal the gem for a Frenchman.

The Case of the Falling Mountain Goat

PART ONE

"Your brother's body was on top of the pile of rope, broken by it. If he had fallen or been murdered whilst climbing, the rope would have fallen with him, or even after him if it was being fastened to the cliff. Either way, it would not have been beneath him. Furthermore, it would have been settling as he landed, and his impact would have spread it out around him, rather than compounded it coiled beneath him. So much for that. Then, if he had attained the top of the cliff and slipped carelessly, the rope would not have come down at all. If he was ambushed on the cliff and thrown off, the rope would, again, have either remained attached or been piled on him, rather than vice versa. No, it is plain that he was met at the top of the cliff by someone whose presence he feared, and that he sent the rope down himself so that, if something happened, an astute investigator would plainly see the foul play."

PART TWO

I saw the answer myself, for once.
Vincent Forster had told us that
the cliff top Enoch had fallen
from was inaccessible without
either climbing up directly or
hiking strenuously through a hilly
forest. Danton blatantly lacked
the muscle to climb a cliff face -
even an easy one - and even had he
possessed the strength of will to
force himself to make a long hike
through adverse terrain, it would
be an incredibly stupid move for
an acute asthmatic. Even assuming
he had met Enoch there, he could
not have overpowered a strong
climber, particularly not one wary
enough to release his descent rope
early as a tell-tale sign in case the
worst happened.

PART THREE

"Honestly, Watson. Vincent
told us at the start that there
was virtually no news or police
interest in the death, and he was
the only one in Enoch's circle
who saw the corpse. He specified
quite plainly that he had not told anyone about the way the limbs had
detached on impact. The only way that Louis Baxter can know of the
dismemberment is if he was there, and thus, he is the killer."

Our testimony was enough to get the police to reopen the case, and
Baxter's paramour of some years finally informed them that she and
Enoch had fallen in love. Their relationship had become physical. She
told Baxter that she was leaving about a week before the murder and
had expected Enoch to propose as soon as was seemly. Faced with this
revelation, Baxter confessed that he had hiked up to the cliff to confront
Enoch and, in the heat of the moment, had thrown him over the edge.

The Phantom of Henwood House

PART ONE

He deduced that the reddened skin over the mouth and nose was a clear indication that a pad of cloth had been clamped over the unfortunate victim's face and held there with sufficient strength to prevent breathing. It takes some minutes to smother someone to death and, even if one takes care to avoid a bruising impact, the redness is unavoidable. There was no other wound, however. If one is lucky, an uninterested doctor seeing the body a day or two after death might well assume the cause to be a heart attack.

PART TWO

"I'll grant you the possibility that the smothering napkin was plucked from Redvers's own rooms, so that is not definitive. But there was glass crushed into the footprint outside the window. If the glass had fallen onto the footprint, it would not be crushed down. So the footprint was made after the window had broken - but its position and direction only makes sense for someone making a careful approach to the door. It was placed there to mislead, as I suspect the body was likewise arranged. Most likely, the killer didn't even break the window until after Redvers was dead. The clear intent is to throw suspicion on some outsider, showing us that the killer is anything but."

PART THREE

Howard went very still when I produced my gun, and he allowed Holmes to truss him like a turkey using some rope he'd spotted on the back of the carriage. "When a man is clearly in two places at once, Mr Howard, I do not cry impossibility, or reach for religious miracles. I look around for his identical twin. The police, shortly, will look for yours and, whichever of you it was who murdered Redvers, the other will swing alongside him for his part in this conspiracy."

As predicted, a quietly hidden twin was located in a secret sub-room in the house. The pair had been planning revenge on Redvers for years because of his very significant role in the suicide of their sister. They had managed to get the job of the man's butler, trading off regularly to ensure no error of individual mannerism betrayed them. They had, in fact, been slowly poisoning the old man with lead and mercury, but Miss Redvers's suspicions and our arrival had made them decide to risk killing him that night. The timing of the party at Uppark was just a useful coincidence.

THE DEATH OF A CRIMINAL

PART ONE

"Look at the floor, man. We can see clearly from the alley that they dragged the corpse out and dumped it in the skip. They may have swept the floor to obscure their boot prints, but they made no effort to disguise this bloodstain. If you drag a fresh corpse, it leaves a trail of blood behind it. There is no blood trail either in the room or in the alley. The body was several hours old before it was dragged out of here."

"He could still have been killed here," Lestrade said, sounding a little hurt. "Maybe they left him on the floor for a while."

"Highly unlikely. Why leave the corpse here and return to move it, or keep guard over it until the blood has settled? It would be a totally unnecessary risk. For that matter, why sweep the floor but not attempt to disguise the drag-marks in the alley or the bloodstain in here? The blood here might be transfer of residual blood from the corpse's skin and clothes, but I suspect that it, too, is a lie - most likely pig's blood. No, this scene is a clumsy attempt to misdirect, which, in turn, informs me that there is useful information to be had at the actual location of the fellow's death."

PART TWO

"My dear fellow, our dubious Mr Fletcher was killed by someone he likely knew and felt comfortable enough with to let his guard down. Almost certainly, that is the principal of the operation, because these groups tend to employ the roughest subordinates. The killer left a footprint behind. A small one. You say you know of two dozen slavers. How many have size-five feet? Yes, a footprint can lie but, almost always, villains disguising their shoe size choose larger shoes, rather than going to the unusual trouble of fitting smaller soles to shoes they can get their feet into."

PART THREE

"My dear Watson, it's perfectly plain. All three took pains to casually work their alibis into their stories, but you must remember that Lestrade told them only that Fletcher was found dead on Monday morning. Whilst Dayson and Harbison established alibis for the entire weekend and more besides, Kenzie only gave herself an alibi for Saturday. This whole case is being kept extremely quiet. Only the killer could know the correct day."

Once he was focused on just one suspect, and with Barings putting pressure on the top brass to resolve this quickly, Lestrade and his men were able to drill down into Helena Kenzie's life and recent activities. It took some time, but they were able to find sufficient evidence to convict her to a lifetime in prison for Fletcher's murder. A number of high-profile government and business resignations followed discreetly behind as her brothels were dismantled. To my dismay, she was not prosecuted for her slavery operation - it was clear that Barings were working behind the scenes to keep the matter quiet - but her victims were, at least, freed.

THE PHANTOM

PART ONE

I had no need of an explanation to share Holmes's scepticism. A man with the dramatic wounds described would be unable to stagger more than a step or two at most before collapsing. The idea that he entered a pub, dragged the landlord out and walked to the alley before speaking and collapsing is pure fantasy.

PART TWO

"You heard the fellow, Watson. A man that tall stands out, and dockyard caulkers and haulers get everywhere in the course of their daily work. His height was in the legs, and they've not seen anyone that height around before or since. Mr Jackson described his walking as 'stalking'. I strongly suspect that his height was mummery - platformed shoes, in all probability. The reality is almost certainly that he's far less distinctive."

PART THREE

"I don't know where the real captain of *Restoration* is, although I expect that there is actually a vessel by that name currently at the docks somewhere. But we certainly did not meet him. No nautical man would ever be so flagrantly incautious as to refer to his ship as 'it'. That is said to be the surest invitation to disaster and, even if the man himself were not superstitious, he would never be able to convince his crew otherwise. Why, even speaking to a potential client in such a manner would be a complete *faux pas*. The man is an imposter, and the death of Simon Brannon is bound up in his lies."

And so it was.

Holmes had the Douglas Nicholson swiftly arrested. His name, it transpired, was Ted Mooney, and he was sought for questioning regarding murders, thefts and fraudulent transactions in cities across the United Kingdom. He'd attempted to disguise himself and defraud Simon Brannon regarding a shipment of marble cladding, but the architect had cottoned on and been killed when he attempted to confront the villain. Ironically, the only reason Mooney was still in Wapping was that another crook was in the process of swindling him with regards to a very valuable but utterly non-existent shipment of stolen gems.

THE BAYLISS KILLINGS

PART ONE

"Honestly, Watson, you, at least, have no excuse for such credulity. The correct volume of blood for the man's body is indicative, yes, but it is hardly proof. It could have come from anyone - an animal, a different person, even the missing man himself if it was extracted over an extensive period of time and kept frozen. Ask yourself this: why would the killer trouble to take the son's body but leave the father's? It is curious. We must restrict ourselves to fact and avoid supposition."

PART TWO

"Watson, stand here in my location a moment, if you will."

I obeyed him, standing in front of the French window.

He opened the door and walked ten feet out onto the lawn. The temperature in the room plummeted. Holmes raised a hand to point at me. "I am a crazed assassin, Watson. I snap a shot at your head from here and miss. Where, pray tell me, does the bullet go once it has whistled past your ear?"

Bayliss and I turned to look at the huge, unblemished expanse of mirror on the far side of the room, and its conspicuous lack of gunshot holes.

"My God," Bayliss said slowly.

"Quite so," Holmes said, coming back into the room briskly and closing the door. "There was no assassin. Your brother fired the gun himself, most probably on the lawn, then dashed back to the door to counterfeit the attack - just as, I am now certain, he counterfeited his own apparent murder."

PART THREE

"Sir," Holmes said, "you are a specialist in transportation. How long does it take to sail from Marseilles to Southampton?"

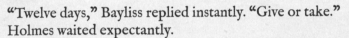

"Twelve days," Bayliss replied instantly. "Give or take."

Holmes waited expectantly.

Wilfred hesitated but then, as he pieced Holmes's thoughts together, said, "So there's no way Glad could have sailed here in four days. She might have used the train, I suppose, but why would she lie?"

"She would not. The nun is your brother Jack," Holmes declared. "He apparently possesses no sense of the time required for travel. Fetch the police. Watson, you have your pistol?"

It took a bit of careful arranging but we managed to isolate the fake nun without causing alarm, and then I held him at gunpoint until the police arrived.

It all turned out to be dreadfully pedestrian, of course. Jack had killed his father in rage at his impending dismissal, then decided to fake his own death to avoid suspicion. But he realized then that he would not be able to claim his share of the will, so he decided his best play was to turn up as his own sister to collect her bequest, under the pretence of aiding the monastery. After that, he'd vanish for good. The real Gladys hadn't even heard of her father's death until Wilfred went to France to find her, but I understand that her mother superior was grateful for the donation.

THE MOST IRREGULAR MR WIGGINS

PART ONE

"Obvious, innit?" Wiggins shot the two policemen a cheeky grin. "No glass out 'ere, none in there neither, and dirty floors in both spots. This window's been empty two weeks or more, going by this 'ere muck. Our manager's either telling you porkies, or 'e ain't even looked at 'is own warehouse in a fortnight - and, either way, that's very interesting, ain't it now?"

"Precisely so, Wiggins," Holmes said. "Would you mind telling the inspector here your age?"

"Well, I ain't exactly certain, given the, er, irregularities of my birth, which I doubt is a surprise to any of you fine gents 'ere, but eleven does seem a likely guess."

PART TWO

"There's splinters all over that tarp," Wiggins said. "Right bleedin' obvious. 'ow exactly do you get splinters from a ripped-open crate on the inside of a tarp that was folded closed at the time? You ruddy well don't, that's 'ow. This robbery stinks like week-old guts."

PART THREE

"They all keep banging on about that window. We know it's not fresh. Impossible, that is, not just unlikely. Manager might, maybe, 'ave missed that with four sites to watch, but the lads 'ere every day wouldn't, not even if they never came down the back - and their cigarette ends say otherwise - not with the weather like this. This entire thing is flimflam. I did enjoy the old boy's performance, though." He broke off to give Inspector Lestrade a meaningful look. "It's so obvious, even a guttersnipe like me can see it."

Lestrade had the whole group rounded up and questioned and didn't darken our door for less than a real emergency for quite some time afterward. All four of the men eventually confessed to having been in on the theft from the start, along with one of the company's coachmen, and the watches were retrieved from a hiding spot in Battersea.

THE WARDEN & THE COACHMAN

PART ONE

Warden looked startled for a moment and then he nodded. "Of course, sir. The shoes."

I blinked and then realized what he meant. The shoes were perfectly clean, soles included, whilst the front of his clothes were absolutely filthy. The body could only have been dumped after he'd been killed.

"Which means," Holmes said, "that we cannot assume he was even in that area before his death."

PART TWO

"You must have seen the scorching on the wound, my dear Watson. That was caused by the real murder weapon, which was red hot. That crude dagger was used afterward in a clumsy attempt to disguise the cause of death. It's eye-catching, but it did not strike the fatal blow."

PART THREE

"Dandison says he saw our mystery man from the back, and that he was wearing a greatcoat, yet he was also able to say that the fellow's shirt was silk and that his suit was an expensive cut? Utter nonsense. He's lying through his teeth, trying get rid of us so he has time to make his escape."

Dandison was arrested, and it eventually came out that he'd been blackmailing Kenneth Riley over a past indiscretion. Riley came past that evening and attempted to reason with him, but the argument escalated and Dandison killed the man with a piece of metal he'd been working that was still hot enough to blacken the wound. He then hastily forged the ugly dagger we'd seen to try to disguise the nature of the stab, and cut the body with it, before dumping the body somewhere disreputable.

THE CASE OF THE INDIAN TIGER

PART ONE

"Look at the chair, my dear Watson. That cut in the back is very unlikely to come about during the course of a brawl. When a man picks up a chair to fend off a knife-wielding attacker, he grips the back and arms, and defends with the legs. One would not hide behind such a thing unless one were a child. It's too small and flimsy a protection. So the cut there is indicative of a quiet assassination - an unexpected knife in the back. This is confirmed by the wounds on the body. There is one stab wound on the back, whilst every other wound is on the front of the body. One does not turn a corpse, or near corpse, over to stab it once in the back. So Albinson was oblivious to the danger when he was stabbed in the back through the fabric of his chair. If he had reacted with strength, he would, in all likelihood, have been stabbed in the back again. Even if the assassin proved suddenly irresolute and permitted the man enough time to stand and turn, he would still have been a man in his mid sixties with an unexpected stab wound. Any ensuing struggle would have been far less destructive than this." He waved his hand around the room. "This is mere camouflage."

PART TWO

"There's no way you saw a specific man across the park at sunset, sir," Holmes said in response the butler's protestations. "The park is to the west, and the sunlight you claim highlighted him would have most certainly been in your eyes. One dark outline at a hundred yards is quite indistinguishable from another. I strongly urge you to tell me the absolute truth if you hope to wrest anything save disaster from this situation."

PART THREE

"I understand why the maid was driven to stab your husband in the back, madam. I also understand why you and Carey went to such pains to stage a plausible fight scene, and I'm quite confident the police will be happy to look no further. However, you should be aware that, when used forcefully, the cross-guard of a dagger leaves a very clear bruise along the wielder's thumb and corresponding part of the hand, and I strongly suggest that, if the police seek to interview the girl, she wear gloves and be ready with another plausible reason for the mark. I do not think they will be needed, but preparation is essential. Now, please, send for your Mr Howe so that Watson and I can be done with this whole sorry affair."

Holmes was as good as his word, I added some plausible-sounding medical jargon, and the lawyer pronounced himself perfectly satisfied that the household was innocent of Albinson's death and that the estate could be bequeathed appropriately. Holmes demanded to know the sum of his fee and, when we got home, declared that he had no interest in blood money, and sent a cheque in that amount payable to the maid.

PICTURE CREDITS

The publishers wish to thank Shutterstock for their kind permission to reproduce all the pictures in this book, with the exception of the following illustrations:

p12 Public Domain, p33 Chronicle/Alamy Stock Photo, p39 Public Domain, p44 KGPA Ltd/Alamy Stock Photo, p46 Library of Congress, p52 Cornell University Library, p59 The Met/Dodge Fund, 1956, p67 Thislife pictures/Alamy Stock Photo, p73 Driftless/Creative Commons Attribution-Share Alike 4.0 International, p97 Allan Cash Picture Library/Alamy Stock Photo, p117 Granger Historical Picture Archive/Alamy Stock Photo, p126 Historic Collection/Alamy Stock Photo, p150 KGPA Ltd/Alamy Stock Photo, p171 Classic Image/Alamy Stock Photo, p179 Public Domain, p181 David Brightmore/Creative Commons Attribution-Share Alike 4.0 International, p182 Jorge Ryan/Creative Commons Attribution-Share Alike 4.0 International.